I0551608

VESTIGE

ALSO BY ANTONIO ROBERTS

The Vestige Saga

Vestige: Rise of the Pureblood

Vestige: What Lies Beneath

VESTIGE

Rise of the Pureblood

ANTONIO ROBERTS

This is a work of fiction. Names, characters, places, and incidents either are the product of the author's imagination or are used fictitiously. Any resemblance to actual persons, living or dead, events, or locales is entirely coincidental.

Copyright © October 2020, second edition, by Antonio Roberts

All rights reserved. No part of this book may be reproduced or used in any manner without written permission of the copyright owner except for the use of quotations in a book review. For more information, email theantonioroberts@theantonioroberts.com

First edition published March 2020. Second edition October 2020

ISBN 978-1-7347426-5-7 (paperback)

ISBN 978-1-7347426-0-2 (eBook)

theantonioroberts.com

CHAPTER ONE

Most turn the other way at the sight of me. Scales were never in style, I suppose. I'm a mistress of my names—I've worn many identities and many lives on this disgusting wasteland we call home. Call me Sinopa, for now. It's the first name I ever knew and where my story begins.

It all started in a tavern. Cliché, right? I can hear the groans now. Out of all the places in the land of Kanaa, it had to be a tavern. Well, I'm sorry but that's just how it is sometimes. Poor expectations bearing poor reality, and vice versa. People can't seem to see past their preconceived misconceptions, and I get that. First impressions are everything—and first impressions of me? Well, let's just say they're not the best.

We served and cooked at the Cat's Meow, a nearby tavern our Aunt Maude owned. Being in Helioshire, it was one of those dingy dives where the food was crap, the people were crap, and—you guessed it— the prices followed suit.

Lanterns at each table lit the interior. Drunks and all breeds of bozos crowded them like moths to a flame. Sadly, even though this was my first night in town, this wasn't my first time working in the restaurant business. I guess I should've known what I was getting into, but I had hoped life would be better on the cusp of the bustling inner city. How wrong I was.

As I threw on my apron I realized that manners and courtesy, even here, were a second language. The clients were just as charming as usual: spitting slurs, drooling, hungover at the bar, and vicious flirting. The naive teenager that I was, I soaked it all in like a sponge.

This was my life. I kept a smile on my face through everything and became a human doormat (or whatever I was because even I didn't know). I suppose it comes with being a foster child as well. I never knew my true age, but I gathered I was seventeen to nineteen years old.

I scrubbed that bar until I could see myself in it. I was young then— bright, bubbly and stupid. My scales glowed in a lustrous cherry-red, and my auburn curls bunched around my horns. Sadly, some patches of hair were hopelessly tangled in knots. I stood a whopping five feet tall, but heels helped.

That night, my foster sister, Angela, manned the kitchen. She said, "Gosh, Sinopa, the place is falling apart as it is. The last thing we need is your cooking." She always was Mother's favorite. *Nice to see you, too.*

Anyway, I had the bar to myself. With a fake smile plastered on my face, I wiped bile and booze off the hardwood bar. I'd spent many a night wiping them beauties.

I gazed out over the floor, looking at the men gathered around eating together; I sighed. As with any dumb teenage girl, relationships mattered. I was alone. Sailors gathered around spinning yarns, fathers and sons bonded over beer, and couples exchanged sweet-nothings.

But love remained elusive for me. I was different, and people treated me as such. The fact is, it was at this very bar that I met the start of my troubles.

A man sat down at the end of the bar with his head on his arm. He held an empty shot glass in his free hand. His hair hung in ferocious amber streaks like a lion's mane. His black frock coat was ragged. It draped long and open with a hood and collar in the back.

"Hiya," I said, waving over his slumped body.

No response.

"Hey, I said 'hello.'"

2

His eyes blinked up at me. They were wild emerald fields.

"Can I get you a drink?"

"No. Now beat it, lizard-wench."

"Sheesh. Friendly, aren't we?"

His head dropped again. Then he said, "I don't wanna hear it. Tell you what, give me the hardest scotch you got. And hold that ice, will you? People around here are cold enough as it is."

I laughed louder than I should have. Maybe it was his striking eyes. As he reclined, drinking his shot, a familiar wooden handle stuck out of his coat.

"I see you have a flintlock there."

He wiped his mouth and closed his jacket. "What of it?"

"Nothing. Just thought it was neat. I have one like it."

"Ha, that's a good one. I'll have to remember that. A scaled beast like you with a sophisticated gentleman's rifle. Boy, that's rich. You're cute, you know that?"

"But it's the truth."

"Look, kid, I don't want to entertain whatever delusions you're having. Leave me alone, capiche?"

"Sorry to bother you, then." I turned to leave.

"Hey, don't walk away. Unless the drink's free, that is?"

"I don't know. Would it bother you too much?"

"You're all right, kid." The man smirked and placed the money on the counter with a modest tip. "Name's Sinopa," I said, extending my hand.

He only nodded, massaging his head.

"It means fox," I said, followed by a hissing sound. "Well, that's not the sound the fox makes, but, uh . . . ." *Totally nailing this.*

The man sighed, still holding his head.

"With all due respect, that's very cute and touching, and you seem like a good girl and all," he burped, "but my head hurts. Please, sweetheart, let a man drink away his troubles in peace."

I apologized and heard my name being shouted in the back of the house. All kidding aside, it turned out that Angela—not me—had started

3

a small kitchen fire, and lucky me would have to explain the long wait to the customer. *Oh, joy.*

I brought out the charred chicken cutlets to the table. The man's face spoke for itself. He wasn't having any of it. His build lumbered tall and thick. His gut curled out a few inches over his waistband.

"Don't tell me I waited twenty minutes for that!" he roared.

"Please, sir, if you'll let me explain—"

"Oi, Shorty! Get a load of this trash!"

An even larger man, this one more muscular, came from the next table beside him. Five behemoths gathered around behind him in a wall of ink, muscle, and dreadlocks. My impulse was to bolt for it.

Why do I have to do this? Angela was the one who burned it, not me.

Angela peeked out the porthole of the kitchen door, giving me a thumbs up.

"I ain't paying for that," Shorty stated.

"Sir, just let me explain—"

"No. Listen here, Goatface. You let me explain. I have been waiting long and hard for this, so get your ugly tail in there and make it right."

"Yes, sir, but—"

He grabbed me by one of my horns and pulled me close. "But what?"

I winced, not bearing to look him in the eye. "But—but—we will get it right."

He flung me onto the floor, knocking the chicken off the table. "See that you do. I'm skin and bones here," he grumbled.

I dusted myself off and muttered under my breath, "Could stand to lose a little to me."

Bam!

Before I knew what hit me, his fist sent me reeling to the floor again. Angela rushed out of the kitchen, no longer standing on the sidelines. Another one of them grabbed her by the throat, lifting her into the air. It was showtime now in The Cat's Meow. Patrons stared motionlessly. A few applauded.

A shadow approached behind me. I scrambled, crawling underneath the tables. Shorty hollered after me. Tables flew, and food with it. Potatoes covered Shorty's shirt. He yanked off a tablecloth and cleaned the mess off his shirt..

That was my chance. I darted under a tablecloth in the corner, hoping to wait it out.

"Where are you?" Shorty screamed.

Footsteps hit the hardwood floor closer and closer. I tucked my head against my knees and held my breath.

Shorty's friend turned over my hiding spot. His boot hit me in the chin and pinned me to the floor.

"Gotcha."

Shorty huffed closer. My tail sucker-punched his friend in the groin. He shrieked and fell to his knees. The patrons winced as if they felt it. I stood baffled. As his friend tried to stand, I swung him back down. My knuckles stung. I kissed and shook my fist.

The crowd roared. Behind me, Shorty charged. He scooped his arms under me and threw me across a table. I groaned to my feet. He swung his fists. I leapt back and wind rushed around my face. Adrenaline pulsed. The fat man huffed.

Holy crap. I dodged that!

I got cocky and swung for his chin. My knuckles cracked. I rubbed my hand. Shorty grinned, kicked me to the ground, then stomped on my throat. "Puny skank," he spat.

I choked, trying to speak. I flicked my tail out of his reach.

"What was that?" he sneered. He raised up his boot so I could speak.

"Big talk for a tub of lard," I managed.

He stomped on my neck again and pushed me further into the floor. A switchblade opened from his shirt pocket. "Try talking without a tongue, snake."

He teased me with the knife and my vision followed it. Out of the corner of my eye, I saw my sister gag as a cohort pushed his elbow down harder on her throat. Her eyes watered and her cheeks turned blue.

A shadow cast over Shorty and nudged his back.

"Let her go and sit down." The voice was calm and plain. It was the man from the bar. Shorty stood up to face him. I caught my breath and crawled to safety. Shorty's cohorts dropped Angela as another reached across the table.

One of them laughed. They charged. The first to swing was thrown to the floor. Shorty moved forward with his knife. The scruffy-faced man kneed him into his last standing man.

A patron from the crowd got brave enough to throw Shorty a sword. The audience would have their blood.

The man from the bar held an unsettling calm as he said, "Put it down and leave now."

Shorty's sword shimmered in the light, "You should've stayed out of this."

He charged.

The scruffy-faced man pulled his flintlock and fired.

BOOM.

The drunk slumped to the floor. The room stopped and stared as the gunshot rang through the air. I had heard nothing like it before. As the smoke cleared from his face, the room was dead silent.

"Anybody got a problem with that?"

There were a few coughs as everyone shook their heads.

He helped me to my feet.

"Thanks for the drink," he said, holstering his gun. And with that, he pushed out the double doors of the bar and never looked back.

CHAPTER TWO

My hounds rushed at the apartment door. I smirked, petting them with one hand and holding my shiner with the other. Angela's scowl was worth every hour of carting them up here this morning.

"Don't think we won't discuss this later," she snapped.

"They're family. The farm's gone. What's there to discuss?" I said.

"Can it. Get out of those clothes. I'll get a kettle going and a compress for your eye."

As I exited the room, Blind Petey whined around Angela, blocking her path to the kitchen. She grumbled, broke down, and petted him. I praised my other partners in crime, hobbling to my room. I would definitely feel sore in the morning. *Some first night here.* My robe, go figure, was at the bottom of my trunk.

Suddenly, the dogs went crazy. All three howled and ran to sound of someone knocking at the front door After restuffing my trunk, I threw on my robe and tiptoed down the hall in my nightgown. It was nearly midnight. The last thing I wanted to do was entertain anyone, let alone Angela's precious "Pookie-Poo."

Angela cursed at the dogs to stay back. The mutts desperately clawed and yelped at the door.

This gift just keeps on giving.

Lucky for her, the door had a chain. I couldn't fathom what her problem was. The geezers would only lick them to death.

"May I help you?" Angela asked, perturbed.

"Yes, ma'am. We're with the authorities. We understand there was a murder in the vicinity and we'd like to ask you some questions."

"Make it quick. I've got a kettle on," she snapped.

I peered around the corner and two armed men in leather uniforms stood outside the open door.

"Yes, ma'am. we know it's late. We were told a 'Miss Sinopa' lives in this building—it was Sinopa, right, Jim?"

His associate nodded. "Any idea where we might find her?"

"What for?" Angela asked.

"Afraid we can't give too many details as it is an ongoing investigation, you must understand, but witnesses described a figure matching her race and build leaving the scene."

"You're wasting your time interviewing her. I was there. The man with the flintlock shot the tub of lard dead as four o'clock."

Jim frantically jotted down every word she said in a leatherbound journal. "This is a separate incident, ma'am."

"What do you mean, 'a separate incident?' She has only been here all evening!"

The officer placed a hand on her shoulder. "Several cases, we believe. Now, this may be hard to understand—"

CRACK!

Angela's hand smacked his away. "Get off me!"

"I meant no offense in—"

"Some taken." She ground her teeth. "Anything else?"

"What is your relationship to the suspect in question?"

"You can't put this on her; she's been with me all evening."

"Innocent until proven guilty, ma'am. Now, your relationship?"

"Her sister. I'm the only family the brat has left."

Jim's pen scratched.

"May we search the premises?"

"You got a warrant?"

"Well, no, but—"

She slammed the door in their faces.

"Thank you for your time," the first man called from the other side.

The floorboards creaked as I crept out to make sure the coast was clear.

"You!" Angela shouted.

I ducked back around the corner.

"Get in here. Sit. Couch. Now."

I did as I was told. Angela spoke like Mom when one of us turds was in for it. The kettle whistled on the stove in a fury of steam.

I sat in silence. My thoughts dreaded every second. What was she going to do with me? What if the police came back? Would they take me away? I was too short to go to prison. I didn't want to know what they did to short girls in prison. And that would only be if I was lucky enough to go to prison for multiple murders.

Angela came back with a cloth of ice and the tray of tea. She bit her lip in the doorway. No fire or malice showed in her eyes, only determination and disappointment. She set the tray down and pressed the ice into my face.

"Stand still."

I winced.

"I said, 'Stand still.'"

She brushed the hair from my face.

"Hurt?"

I nodded, snatching the ice pack away from her.

"Good. Maybe you'll think twice before opening that yap of yours. Come on, Sinopa. You're crazy, you know that?"

The ice numbed my temple and eye socket. My good eye turned to the red finger markings on Angela's throat.

"How's your neck?" I asked.

"You mean besides the fact that I believed my head would explode? Fantastic."

"Sorry."

"Sinopa, what am I going to do with you?" Angela set down her tea, barely touched. "I need to know. Did you do it?"

"Do what?" I asked.

"Two policemen just came to my apartment. What else, smart one?"

"Take it easy."

"What else did you think I was talking about?"

"Okay, sorry. Sheesh. No, I didn't do it. I walked with you the whole way home. Chill, will you?"

Angela sighed with her hands on her head. "What would Mom say? She always knew just the right thing to say."

From the moment I entered, the old lady permeated through Angela's home. She haunted the place, and there was no escaping her. She was in the portraits, decor, and furniture; everything reeked of her. It stank with her old shrew musk of pantyhose, talcum powder, and mothballs. Neither of us would admit it but we both wished Mom were there.

Angela rested her head on my shoulder and sobbed, "Now I'll lose you, too."

I pulled her close.

"There's gotta be some way we can prove I'm innocent."

"Face it, it's hopeless. What will you do? Where will you go? They'll come back with a warrant, ya know. Why'd you have to ruin this for us, Sinopa?"

"You can't blame this on me."

"This was our chance, our dream. We'd live on easy street, save our coin, and one day we'd be inside that golden gate."

"So it's my fault I look like this?" I asked, pointing to the mirror across the way.

I never felt I saw myself in my reflection. I didn't look like anyone else.

Staring back in the mirror at me was a short red figure in a silk night-gown. A plum-colored bruise masked one of her sapphire cat eyes. Her smooth cheeks glistened pink and puffy, scaled in snakeskin. Two fangs protruded from the puckered lip of her scowl. She ran her fingers through her muddy auburn hair. It was impossible to hide her horns, curving in ivory like a ram's. And as if that wasn't enough, a long skinny tail taunted her from behind her back, coiled like a chameleon's.

"You think I enjoy looking like this? I was supposed to reinvent myself here."

"Some reinventing. The serial killer label must look fabulous on your résumé."

Tears began to trickle down my cheeks.

"Hey, I didn't mean it."

"I'm a monster."

Angela rubbed my back as I sobbed. "You're not a monster," she said.

"Well, that's the thing. I don't know what I am. I brought this on myself. I am a monster. It's all my fault."

"Hey." Angela snapped her fingers. "Look at me. Hey. Look at me, sweetie." She grabbed my face in her hands and wiped my cheeks. Angela's lips pursed and her soft green eyes stared back at me. Her brown bangs sat above her eyes. I remember growing up how she had made me feel normal like her—human.

"None of that was your fault. You can't blame yourself for what those jerks did to you, okay? Not them at the bar, not those pigs as a kid, not no one. You got that?"

I nodded.

"Good, now give me a hug; I want to go to bed."

I wrapped my arms around her and squeezed. She had a point, although I would never admit it. A broken clock is right twice a day, I suppose.

"Don't worry over looks so much. We'll figure this out in the morning," she said, letting go.

I dried my eyes.

Angela told me to turn off the light when I was ready to go to bed. I sat on the couch alone and sipped my tea, now lukewarm. My tail swaddled my legs.

I knew her words were true, but it wasn't the easiest thing for my stubborn teenage self to swallow. My words continued to haunt me—I was a monster, a freak, and no one would ever love me.

EVEN NOW, it is difficult to talk about myself and my past. I am not that girl anymore. There are so many things I would love to tell my younger self about: the adventures, the lovers, the travels, things that actually matter in life . . . but if it really came down to it, I probably wouldn't say anything. I'd just plop down beside her, hold her hand, and tell her everything will be okay. But, just maybe she should pack an extra pair of undies, because by midnight . . .

KNOCK, KNOCK, KNOCK.

Our world was about to change.

CHAPTER THREE

There was another knock at the door in the dead of night. I jumped in my skin. My heart pounded. I dared not move a muscle.

KNOCK, KNOCK, KNOCK.

There it was again, this time softer. My curiosity got the better of me.

"Who is it?"

No response.

"Angela? This isn't funny. I know where you sleep."

A moment passed with nothing but silence. Seconds felt like minutes. My eyes scanned for any of the dogs. The ungrateful brats must have been sleeping on my bed. I was all alone.

This better not be the police back with a warrant.

I checked the chain before cracking open the door.

I called into the dark hallway.

Obscured in the shadows was the figure of the scruffy and green-eyed man who saved me at the bar.

"Miss Sinopa, I presume?"

"Yes?" My voice shook.

"May I come in? There's something I wish to discuss, and I'm afraid it can't wait till morning."

I nodded, shut the door, and undid the chain.

He walked in, and I gestured to the couch for him to sit down. My nerves stirred restlessly.

Could I trust him? What if he was the murderer out to get me next?

I had seen what he was capable of, and here I was defenseless in my jammies. There was no way my bunny slippers could spring to my defense should things turn sour.

I offered him the tea on the table and he poured himself a cup. His face puckered. Given how bitter Angela liked her tea, I couldn't blame him.

I twitched and shivered in my chair across from him. "You said there was something you wanted to discuss."

"Yes. You mentioned earlier you had a flintlock pistol?"

"So now you believe me?" I laughed.

"No."

I frowned.

"But I'm looking for someone. And seeing how you're the only lead I have, here I am."

His voice was smooth and proper, like the Queen's English, yet his appearance was that of a vagabond or a castaway sailor.

I had never had such an interesting house guest.

I teased, "So, who is it—your girlfriend or something?"

His eyes turned to the floor.

"You could say something like that." He let out a long sigh. "Normally, though, the women chase me. Not the other way around."

I rolled my eyes.

"Can't this wait until morning?"

"Afraid not. I best be moving on. A man's dead, thanks to you."

"Me? Whatever. Wait here." I walked back to my room and pulled open my trunk.

Nestled like a chocolate egg lay a small, ornately carved walnut handle with a cold iron barrel, swaddled in a blanket. It rested right where I had left it, untouched for so long. It was my greatest treasure and one of my few possessions from childhood.

I came back and handed him the gun.

Immediately, he put down his cup and spent five minutes turning

14

over the weapon. He inspected every inch of the contraption: the barrel, the stock, and the markings, like a jeweler scrutinizing the cut of a gem. His eyes couldn't contain their excitement.

I stood tall, proud of my treasure.

"Yup, that's his work all right," he said, passing me back the grip.

"Who?"

"The same one who made mine."

Then he pulled a similar pistol out of his coat. It was smaller in the barrel. The wood splintered and flaked in places, and the markings appeared worn off.

"When did you get yours?" he asked.

"When I was little. Maybe about seven years ago. A nice man gave it to me."

"What did he look—wait, he gave a child one of these?"

Truthfully, I had never thought of it that way before.

"I wasn't that little."

"Well, how old were you?"

"Well, let's see . . . I'd be . . . I—"

"You mean you don't know?" he interrupted. At this point, he began getting pushy for the details.

"Of course I do!" I said defiantly, placing my hands on my hips.

To this day, I'm not sure how old I am. Birthdays before my foster mother weren't the most special. With my upbringing, I based everything off of Angela being the same age as me. More likely, she's five years my elder, but that's beside the point.

"I was ten!" I lied.

"Whatever. It doesn't even matter if it was him. It was too long ago." He stood up, ready to leave. "Thank you for your time."

"Wait!" I called out. "Where are you going?"

"Aerogapolis, where else? The only place left to search for a lead."

"Take me with you."

"Why would I do that?"

"I . . . uh . . . because you owe me."

He chuckled to himself.

"Funny, I don't seem to recall owing you anything. You owe me for not letting that swine bash in the rest of your pretty face."

"I showed you the gun. Please, I need to get out of here. I'd like to see the big city. Talk is that there are others like me there. I want to see where I came from and who I am."

"I'm not running a daycare here, let alone a travel service," he said.

The man started making his way to the door.

I called out after him, "Wait! Please don't go. I need your help. I'll do anything. Maybe I scratch your back, you scratch mine. Remember the guys at the bar, right?"

"Get on with it. The police are crawling out there."

"Well, they're after me, too."

The man turned around and crossed his arms. "What's your offer?"

"I'll cook. I'll clean. I can do anything. Please, just don't leave me here."

"No. Money, kid. How much?"

"I don't have any money."

"That's what I thought." He took another step toward the door.

"Please, I'll do anything. Name your price; I'll work it off. If you'll help me prove I'm innocent, I'll help you find your girlfriend. Anything."

He sighed. "Your flintlock."

"What?"

"You said anything, right? Throw in your flintlock, you got yourself a deal."

He came back and paced around me and the coffee table like a shark. I looked down at the grip sticking out of my robe pocket.

"But this is special, and—"

"You named your price, kid: *anything*. Remember? It's the gun or the trip, sweetheart. You decide."

My eyes remained fixed on my treasure.

I hardly know him, and this is worth a fortune—at least, I think. Regardless, it's worth more than money to me. It's my only clue to my past. My last trinket from my home. If I leave, wouldn't that show guilt?

One of the dogs whined down the hall and scratched at Angela's door.

"Well, kid, I'm waiting."

"I'm thinking."

"Well, think faster."

If I stay, I might get Angela involved. I can't bear to see her hurt because of me. Do I really have a choice?

I sighed. "Take care of it, will you?"

I gingerly placed my greatest treasure in his hands.

"You have my word." He extended his other hand. "Do we have a deal?"

How do I know he won't take my pistol and run? But if I don't take the risk, can I really outrun the police alone? I don't even know the city. Decisions. Decisions.

"You swear you'll help me prove my innocence?"

"I'll do my very best."

What am I saying? This is the guy who saved my life. Possibly Angela's, too. That seems trustworthy enough.

I closed my eyes, shook his hand, and nodded.

"Splendid. Now, we have plenty to discuss. But for now, pack light. We leave in the morning. That's dawn, before sunrise, is that understood?"

I nodded.

"Good. Now one more thing." He handed me a thick wrinkled book.

"*The Big Book of Baby Names*? I think you have the wrong idea."

"If you want to be free of this place, you need a new name. Trust me, kid. That's one thing you don't want to hold you back."

"That's stupid. I'm not changing my name."

"I just shot a man. It'd be best you change your identity if you want to accompany me. Take my word on it. It doesn't matter what you pick, just so long as you remember and stick to it. This is how I keep track of who I've been."

"So, what's your real name?"

"That's a personal question. I don't answer those. My alias is secret for the time being. I've used many. See for yourself."

I weighed the weathered book in my hands. Pages inside buckled with creases and dog-eared corners. Ink crossed out or checked off nearly every name. A white feather bookmarked the first page I opened. My eyes began going over the names. Two different color inks lined each page: red for the girls and black for the boys. In the center was one untouched minus a heart beside it: *Kiera.*

"See any you like?"

"How 'bout Kiera?"

"Any name but that one."

"What? Why?"

"Just pick another name," he snapped.

"Why? You said it didn't matter."

His jaw and fist clenched and he shook his head as he exhaled.

"Whatever. Just think it over. I'll meet you in the stables before sunrise. You best get some rest."

The door shut behind him without the slightest sound.

He hadn't entirely lied to me about looking for his girlfriend. No, like any good silver-tongued swindler, he chose not to correct me. It was his calling card.

But I was nothing more than a naïve young girl enthused about a chance to fall in love and escape to the big city. The green-eyed man and his promises danced like fireflies in my eyes. Adventure, romance, danger—comes from reading too many books, I suppose. My room was littered with them in my little hideaway at the farm. Had anyone found out, we'd have been on the streets.

I stayed up late in my bedroom that night, turning over the pages and wondering what new persona I would don. Would I reinvent myself as someone elegant and classy, like a Genevieve or a Maybelline? Perhaps something seductive or sexy, like a Roxanne or Zelda? Lola?

None of them were me no matter how much I pretended. Why couldn't I just be me? More and more I kept coming back to that name.

Why not Kiera? It was one of the few not crossed off. The others made me sound like an old lady. Nobody wants to be an Iola or a Maude or a—yuck—Winifred.

CHAPTER FOUR

I'd had the name Sinopa as long as I could remember, even before Angela and I were taken in by our foster mother. I hadn't always lived in Nantucket village. That's right, Nantucket. Get your limericks out now. Tell me one I haven't heard before. Most are only half true.

It was by no means the best place to live. Nestled beside the Fillesterre River it made for a great trade port, but bad for everything else. Crime became commonplace. The farming community didn't stand a chance and the "law enforcement," if they could even be called that, were easily bribed for the right price.

But it wasn't all bad. In fact, I had lived in worse.

To the north, along the river and through the crevice of the Zaku mountain pass, was a small goblin village. In goblin language, my native tongue, the name of the village means "home of green pasture." From the ground rose many small, ramshackle wooden huts, a few teepees, and massive stone fire pits—well, massive by our approximation, of course.

The village extended into the forest with rope bridges and there were towering treehouses for the likes of the chief himself. I never left the ground floor, not if my Pop-pop could help it. Havish stood a staggering total of three feet tall. His wrinkles folded into a warm evergreen color, encroached by a puffy cotton candy beard. He was my only sunshine in that place. My earliest memory was of scooting around his floor. He'd always fuss, "Sinopa, slow down! You're gonna wear down my floor."

I'd always scowl with a, "Yes, Pop-pop."

He was my Pop-pop, and for a while, we did everything together. From playtime, to snack time, to bedtime, it was just the two of us. Then I grew bigger and the visitors came. I couldn't play with Pop-pop when he talked with them outside. I remember one night after supper, he said he had to go to a tribe meeting and I couldn't come.

"Why not, Pop-Pop? I'm a big girl now," I said adamantly, at that time standing a foot taller than Havish himself.

"Now, now, Sinopa. I'm sure you'll have your day, but as for now, I need you to stay here, okay? Everything's going to be all right."

"What do you mean, 'everything will be all right?' Why wouldn't it be?"

The wrinkly goblin stuttered with his words for a second.

"Promise me you'll stay here for the night, okay?"

I nodded, and he kissed my forehead.

He stuck his head in the door one last time before leaving.

"Goodnight. I love you, sugarplum," he said as he shut the door.

I lay in bed tossing and turning. My little red feet stuck out the end of the goblin-sized bed. I had cut my feet out of the footed-pajamas for this very reason. After waiting until I no longer heard footsteps, I rolled out of bed and peeked out the bay window. Havish slowly jabbed his cane into the ground as he shuffled toward the center of town. I rushed down the stairs, intent to follow. The door flung open with no care for stealth. No one appeared to notice.

The mud outside the house squished between my toes. Pop-pop was too poor to buy me shoes. He gave up his own until I outgrew them. I splashed in a few puddles for a while, completely forgetting my mission.

In the distance, drums thundered. I jumped in my skin. Goblin folk left their homes and headed toward the center of town. I remembered the meeting. I toward walked to the square with everyone else. The air was thick and exhilarating after the previous night's rainfall. I had hardly been outside. Pop-pop kept telling me I was sick. I didn't feel sick, though. But he wouldn't let me go outside.

The frigid night air gushed through the trees. I shivered in my pink, footless pajamas. Pop-pop always said these were special. I could never imagine why. The only thing I saw special was a hole for my tail, which by this age swirled out like a pink pigtail. That's what made them my favorite.

The drums beat louder and louder. As I approached, the ground shook with my every step. In the open stone square, a large circle formed. Five robed men stood on stools, banging drums taller than themselves. The chief sat on a chair in the center overlooking the circle.

I sat on the porch of someone's house close enough to see. The drums began beating faster and faster.

M-ba-bum-ba, BUM-ba-bum-ba, BUM-ba-bum-ba.

Louder and louder.

BUM-ba-bum-ba! BUM-ba-bum-ba! BUM-ba-bum-ba! BOOM!

The drums stopped in harmony. All eyes turned to the chief.

His voice rasped in hisses and growls to his people before him, a bowl of green- and grey-skinned goblins.

Goblin doesn't translate very well, so you are going to have to forgive me here. It's beautiful in its simplicity and screeches. It's very blunt and affectionate as you pour emotion into your words. Goblins can be very sentimental, and their language reflects it.

"My people! Big Chief make old Havish come to my great circle. Today enormous havoc in my wondrous village, yes? Havish rescues outsiders. Havish good, yes?"

The circle nodded and clapped before Big Chief lifted his hand for them to stop.

Big Chief continued, "Havish's wife die. Havish wife no more. Big Chief no like treason against my people. Big Chief act kind with Havish. Big Chief let outsider stay, but now time passed. More seasons than Big Chief's toes pass, seasons beyond measure. Outsider still no goblin."

"She's my daughter," cried Havish.

"You raise, yes, but daughter, no. Outsider rocketed tall, taller than goblin. Outsider scary, very dangerous."

"She's never hurt anyone. She'd never hurt anyone."

"Enough! Either she goblin, slave, or outsider. Outsider too big to feed. Too big to control!"

I clenched my knees on the porch. What did they mean I was different? I was one of them. What else would I be?

"Big Chief the benevolent bring to vote. He hear goblins speak, then Big Chief decides."

The crowd murmured to themselves. Tears streamed down my cheeks. I was cold, scared, and tired. I wanted my Pop-pop.

I stood up to walk home. As I did, the porch door swung open.

The goblin lady screamed, "Monster! Monster! Monster on my porch!"

The crowd turned to see me towering in the open. I half ran for the trees. The stronger men unsheathed their scimitars.

I bolted. I ran to the only place I knew was safe. I raced through the crowd toward my Pop-pop.

Everyone pushed and shoved. Red clay clouded the night air. Elbows jabbed everywhere. Those who tripped were trampled. The few women clung to the nearest child they could. It was like someone had set fire to an anthill.

I saw Pop-pop turn and look. I was almost there. There was a shout. My legs fell from under me. My face planted in the sand. Men with scimitars stood over me. Pop-pop yelled for them not to hurt me.

Big Chief roared, "Cursed be outsider! Outsider still no goblin. Outsider will never be goblin. She will be lowest of slaves. Much money shall come to my people and to Big Chief."

The men in scimitars dragged me away. I cried for my Pop-pop as my heels dug in the mud.

He called back, "Sinopy! Sinopa! Oh, my Sinopa!"

"Hey, Sinopa, wake up!" a voice called.

Someone shook me by my shoulders. I awoke, flailing, smacking my head into Angela's above me. She took a step back, staring at me. Her eyes seemed worried again. My heart still raced. My bangs stuck with sweat to my face

"Bad dream?" Angela said, looking over me.

I nodded.

"You wanna talk about it?" she asked.

I shook my head. I could never tell her what happened. I could never tell anyone what happened.

CHAPTER FIVE

After reassuring Angela—because I was "screaming like a friggin' maniac"—I left. I was not screaming, by the way.

I can't say it felt good to sneak out. Growing up, I always hated it when others left without saying goodbye. They didn't have the choice, though. It was their time. Now, look at me. I have no excuse; look at me doing it. If I'm not careful, I'll follow in their footsteps entirely.

Having Angela following me, on the other hand, was a risk I couldn't take. We were sisters, after all. Good or bad, somebody had to have her back, and I couldn't bear the thought of seeing her hurt. I thought my housewarming present—the dogs—should keep her plenty of company in the meantime.

Outside, mist sprang from the arid canyon peaks. The predawn slums rested still and cold. In the daytime, the beggars, the undesirable and the deplorable, lined the road for just a taste, just a peek of what's beyond the gates of Aerogapolis itself. Not many could enter the city back in those days.

The wind gusted through my blouse. My scales rose on end. I never knew a desert could be so cold. The streets remained motionless and empty of any life. Not a single soul dared disturb the silence of the hallowed alleys—except me, the demoness of the night. My heels clicked on the cobblestone walk. Boarded windows whistled with every gust. My bones nearly froze.

I looked over my shoulder and shivered, but the fog obscured anything past twenty feet. Yet, I swore someone or something was watching me. The breeze blew briny and musky. It was almost beastly. Strands of hair brushed on my neck as if they were whispering in my ear, reaching, calling, but there was no one there.

I thought I was just being paranoid. This was the life of a fugitive— always checking over my shoulder, chasing shadows and ducking into them. Dreams of life in the city became nightmares.

Some paradise.

My sack of clothes grew heavy over my shoulder. I debated pulling out another layer but thought better of it. It was late, and who knew what roamed about this side of town? It was best to keep walking. My heels clacked with a purpose. *Would it have killed Angela to buy a pair of flats?* It's not like *I* could afford them.

The road wound and turned in darkness. The stone turned to dirt, and dirt to sludge. I had to be nearing a barn soon. Down the hill, frosty desert sage, winecups and cactus dotted the landscape. Nestled on the edge was a large barn. A faint light shone through the window.

The sun hadn't risen yet when I reached the stables. Inside, the man from the bar sat on a stool with his back toward to me. THUNK. A knife rocketed end over end into a barrel. He threw several more one-by-one. Each sunk another inch from the last. I cleared my throat as I entered.

"You're late," he said, without turning around.

His blades sunk, splintering the wood with hard, hollow cracks. To the side were larger blades, sunk deeper into a support beam.

"I'm sorry. I overslept,. It won't happen again."

"No. No, it won't."

THUNK. Another blade stuck into the wood.

"Oh, come on, please say you'll take me. I said I'm sorry, sir. It won't happen again. Promise."

"Sir?" the man laughed.

You haven't told me your name yet. What am I supposed to call you?

"You're all right, kid. You're just lucky the law's bribe is cheap if I had run into trouble. A deal's a deal. You packed your stuff?"

I lifted my bag up in reply. It took a moment to realize his back was to me and he couldn't see it.

He turned.

"What happened to 'pack light?'"

"This *is* light. Only what I can't live without."

"Whatever. Fetch me those out of the post, will you?" he said, pointing to the center beam in the room.

I nodded and pried the long daggers out of the wall. I gathered at least seven daggers from one of the support beams. The man picked up the smaller knives from the barrel and grabbed his coat from a thick bed of straw. Judging by how it lay, he had slept there.

I clumsily carried the bunch over to him. "You sure you got enough?"

"In my line of work, you can never be too careful. You have my book?"

I pulled *The Big Book of Baby Names* from my coat pocket.

"Good," he nodded. "Have you decided?"

I dug a hole in the dirt with the front of my shoe.

"Is 'Kiera' okay?"

He sighed. "Suppose it has to do. Just as adamant as she was about it," he mumbled. "Stick to it, will you? You play your role, I'll play mine, understood?"

"And you are?"

"Romero. Romero Estaban. That's not my real name, but that's what you shall know me by. I am a trader and you are one of my hired hand-maidens."

"So, I'm supposed to pretend to be your slave?"

"No, you're a handmaiden. There's a difference, trust me. Just follow my lead and you'll be fine. Now let's get going."

Scanning across the empty stables there wasn't a single horse in sight.

"Where's your carriage?"

"Who said anything about a carriage? The front gate's out of the question if that's what you're wondering. You're a wanted man now, remember? Well, woman, but you get the picture."

He pulled a key from his pocket and made his way to another section of the barn. The section appeared to be nothing more than a wall. He ran his hands up across its surface.

"What's this?" I asked.

A small metal rod clinked out of view, and a large wooden door creaked open. "Tools of the trade, my dear."

He pulled down a small oil lantern that had been hanging from a nail by the door and lit the way. Behind the false wall ran a long corridor with stables twice as wide. "Stolen racehorses, bootleg liquor, and anything worth hiding for the right price is all here—where I secured ours."

Armed watchmen checked his deposit slip and kept a close watch as we left.

In the darkened stalls, booths of sleeping black-market traders lined the entrance. Straw and thatch lined the walk. Soon it declined beneath the earth into the literal criminal underground.

Most stalls were as Romero said. Prostitutes and mercenaries chatted in candlelight soliciting each other's services. Bootleg liquor barrels were piled high. Pungent manure and ammonia hit us as we continued further. Goats, horses, and whole carriages secreted themselves in the shadows. In one stall, a crusty, unkempt vagabond slept on a bed of hay. Another held an unconscious man cuffed to the wall. Dried blood on his shirt.

"Just tend to your own business, and they will theirs," Romero warned.

This was my first lesson in thievery: eye contact. A low profile is key to survival.

Our "deposit" was deep in the bowels of the barn. Romero explained how items were safest here, although the premium placement came with a hefty fee. I came upon it there the first time, the Sirius.

A dull lantern glow shone off the metal bird laid before me in the bed of straw. Its wings stretched wide from one end of the stall to the other— about a twenty foot span. Double-ended propellers stood upright out of both wings like dumbbells. On each side, two wings stacked on top of each other connected with spruce struts. The cigar body hung together ramshackle-like with pieces of scrap wood and rusty aluminum patching dents.

Looking back, it really was a death trap even then.

"I call her the Sirius, my wishing star," Romero said, rubbing off the loose straw.

"You have an airship. It must have cost you a fortune!"

"Well, I got it for a steal. Help me push this thing out of here, will you?"

I grabbed hold of one side while he pushed the other. Wide-rimmed carriage wheels rolled in the front and two smaller wheels skirted in the rear. Let me tell you, that thing was *heavy*. Whew-wee! Of course, the straw and the narrow aisle didn't help. The wheels wanted to skid in the turn out of the stall. A good ten minutes and a barrel of sweat later, it was out of the barn.

The airship was much different in dawn's light, which almost gave a little hominess to it. The leather seats appeared hand sewn. The tail proudly displayed the Sirius star and the Northstrand flag.

Carved into the wooden tail, initials spelled "L. H. + E. P." surrounded by a heart.

"Hey, kid—I mean Kiera. Wake up. Put your load in the back and let's get going."

Two seats were bolted into the cigar body, single-file: one for the driver, one for the passenger, with a small space for luggage. When Romero said to pack light, he meant it. The second seat was piled high with burlap sacks full of food and clothes.

Outside, the dawning sun had barely met the tree line. Luckily, it was still too early for anyone to be out and about their business, especially on this side of town. The airship was a thousand times easier to push on flat ground.

"How does it work?" I asked.

"Buckle in and I'll show you."

I looked at the dented metal body and bit my lip.

"Unless you're having second thoughts, that is."

I fumbled over my words, mostly mumbling nonsense.

"Stop, stop. Give me your hand."

I reluctantly held it out. He gently balled it up.

"I want you to do something for me, okay? Take your fist and throw it."

I limply cast my fist in front of me.

"That was weak. Again."

I punched the air in front of me once more.

He grunted.

"We'll have to work on that."

"What was wrong with that?"

"You need to be stronger. Say what you mean and mean what you say. You want to go, don't you?"

"Yes, but—"

"Then show me."

I grabbed onto a truss, hopped into the second seat, and threw another punch. Romero smiled. He followed and helped me with my harness. His body kneeled in close. He snugged the belt tight around my waist. *It's a shame someone snagged him before I could.* My cheeks flushed.

"Right. Now, you see those circles on the wings?"

Two metal dishes were carved in the wings. A large metal track with a series of small onyx-colored blades connected to the outside of the circle. The propeller rod ran between these blades connected by a series of gears.

"It's powered by the mysts," Romero said.

See back in those days, back in my day, the ground sprang up with the mysts of the ancients, the sign of the last mushroom war of the ancients. In caves, low elevation, and darkness, the mysts rose. They produced the magic and monsters of the world. According to the founders of our nations, they were our curse for the "forbidden" pursuits —mainly war, machina, science, and religion.

Personally, I was never one for politics. Nantucket stayed relatively untouched by wars and the authorities of the outside world.

Romero leaped into the cockpit and pulled a lever. A metal cage with three similar beams of onyx clamped down onto the circle in the wing. The circle growled and revved, forming a myst engine. A light fog channeled from the air. A gray cyclone danced and wrapped around the pole.

The cage turned, and the propellers whirled. Romero pulled a lever that engaged the back tail's propeller.

My seat rocked from side to side like a canoe. The Sirius began to rise and rise, until we were ten feet off the ground, then twenty.

"Hang on," Romero yelled over the rotors.

CLICK.

The cages lifted.

SCREAK.

The poles tilted.

The Sirius shot forward, and I screamed. We had liftoff. The ship streaked across the sky, and my stomach stayed behind. We rose higher and higher. The clouds came closer.

The gust was ferocious. My hair batted against my shoulders, and the air ran thin. I had felt nothing like it. I jostled unsteady and wanted to hurl. Sirius was a fine old girl once I gave her the chance. As you'll see, that didn't come easy.

CHAPTER SIX

R omero never let it go that I'd screamed at takeoff. He constantly teased me for it for years to come, and the subject became a sure-fire way to get my tail in a knot.

The air crashed against the Sirius's smooth metal hide, and it really did a number on my hair. I soon took a note to tie my hair up next time so it wouldn't be in knots around my horns.

The view, though. *The view*. It was astounding.

Words didn't do justice to the sunrise from up there. The clouds glowed underneath like tufts of fresh spring magnolia petals, dawn's light dyeing them cotton candy pink. The sky—blends of blue, fuchsia, and rosy lavender.

All was quiet up there, nothing but the buzz of the rotors and the clouds to keep us company. It was peaceful—once we got used to it, that is. The luggage crammed me in tight. My knees dug into Romero's seat in front of me, and don't get me started on the cold.

Romero called me a "first-time flyer" and a "ninny." One of those is true.

I jumped when we hit turbulence. Romero said I "squealed." I didn't squeal, but I clenched my seat for dear life. It was a long way down and there was not a chance I wanted to fall out of that death trap.

He complained, "Quit sinking your claws into the leather. You're tearing up my seat."

For the record, I didn't have claws yet. I stared down beneath me and saw little heads of broccoli strewn across the land, the trees seemed so tiny from where we were. My eyes darted back to my feet. I wasn't having any of it.

"You just focus on flying better. Don't crash this thing, or turn upside down, or whatever."

"You mean like this?"

He nudged the wheel slightly, and the bird began to tilt. I clenched the seat harder.

"No, no, no!" I cried.

With a whoosh, I screamed. My body tensed. My eyes closed. Nothing but the harness held me inside. My hair hung upside down.

"Turn it back! Turn it back!"

The plane tilted upright, completing its full circle. I opened my eyes to see Romero turned around with a brilliant smirk on his face. I may have been breathing heavily, but the air was light, okay?

I crossed my arms and glared at him.

I wanted to kill him. I wanted to skin him alive right there with no regrets. In fact, as soon as he turned around, I slapped him.

"Don't do that!" I shouted.

He doubled over as I wailed on him.

Long story short, my first experience with airships wasn't the best. I learned how to throw a punch then. That's for sure.

I sulked until I saw the city in the distance. Beneath us, the orchards turned sparser to scorched clay savannah. Palm trees rose, replacing the coniferous firs, and even less familiar olive and pomegranate trees.

From the red dirt, the land began to incline. Rivers flowed into the ocean, dividing the inclines into sandy layered canyons and dark stone chasms. Cliffs stood tall and curved, miles above the waves. Aerogapolis sat here.

On cliffs high above the water, the city stretched across the tallest chasm. Helioshire on one side, and Aerogapolis on the other, protected and isolated from the outside world. Wooden suspension bridges stretched across the chasms.

Along the beach stood the Cornerstone Arch community. Wooden plank pathways descended its charcoal colored cliffs in a zig-zag pattern toward the water and docks. Large lighthouses and windmills lined the beach, and smaller windmills dotted the city. Buildings reached for the sky.

"Quite a sight, isn't it?" Romero asked.

A large marble dome with a clocktower at the top conquered the hillside. Two long banners draped both sides of a long tunnel extending from a strip of steel and alien lights. It appeared like a massive igloo.

"Hang on."

CREAK.

Romero pulled a lever.

Before I could even respond, we were falling. Down, down, down. Plummeting like a rock.

The roar of the engines muffled my words. Another lever.

CRACK.

The poles turned. The Sirius's back wheels touched down. Its nose stayed in the air. Each light passed us in blinks.

SCREAK.

The propellers slowed. Sirius continued to barrel into the tunnel. The mouth opened empty and black. The runway turned to marble.

Luckily, a brick wall stood at the end of our path. The clock ticked. Romero pulled another lever. The wheels wobbled and the plane shook from side to side. Walls raced closer. Our wheels skidded. The Sirius chugged. The propellers slowed.

Two men approached with chocks for the wheels, another with a bucket of water. I squeezed Romero's headrest, unable to watch. I felt the Sirius jar back and forth . . . and stop.

I opened my eyes in disbelief. My heart pounded in my chest. Adrenaline coursed through my veins. My body slumped back in the seat. I was alive. Terrified, but alive.

Romero turned around, "You okay back there?"

"Let's do it again!"

Romero laughed.

Larger airships lined the building. The Sirius appeared miniature in comparison. Sections of the floor rotated and spun, making for easier takeoffs and maintenance on a single runway. It was like one modular whirligig on a massive scale. I gazed at it in wonder.

Romero hopped out and sweet-talked the landing crew to take care of the plane. Apparently, this was a lower profile than entering the front gate. Most airships were cargo fleet or a rich merchant's toy. Romero taught me his craft and showmanship.

We always had to be on the lookout for trouble. Too many "fans," as he called them. Yeah, right. Bounty hunters more like it. But I didn't know that at the time. Gosh, I was so stupid. So enamored by the city, I suppose.

After arrangements were in order, I practically dragged Romero out the front gate.

"Just a minute."

"What? Why?"

"Remember, keep your head down, okay?"

I rolled my eyes.

He continued, "Just keep in mind that not everything is as it seems. It's a big city. People aren't always the nicest. What's your name again?"

"Kiera," I said, almost unsure myself.

"Good girl. You'll do fine. Coin purse in the front where you can see it. Stay close."

Only, I didn't catch that last part. As giddy as a schoolgirl, I darted off into the early market square. The roads curved in sandstone brick. Stone and brick encompassed everything.

I shivered and sucked in the sights and smells. Fresh apples, morning loaves of bread, and salty sea breeze drifted through the walls. The sun had only just risen moments before. The wind tunneled through the dimly-lit streets. Not a single streetlamp here.

All the buildings reached, pulling the heavens down in magnificent multicolored stone. Bands of granite, brick, and marble stacked on top of each other. Amazingly, there was no mortar between the bricks. They seemed so old.

Vendors lined the street, stocking their wares with rich and earthy spices. Hefty perfumes permeated the air. I felt dragged by my nostrils.

As I approached the booths, church bells rang in the distance. A merry tune chimed as the wind whistled by the weathered windows. The sun-beaten buildings spread shadows in the side streets and alleyways. Intricately chiseled arches and ancient stone weaved around me in a labyrinth. It soon became clear to me that I was lost.

Suddenly, masses of people marched down the road toward me. Several others joined and locked hands. Songs began to rise, and they matched the merry tune. I stood frozen as the flock of people swarmed.

Before I could step aside, it was already too late. They were upon me. An elderly lady grabbed my hand and a man in white and scarlet robes clenched my other.

"Let go of me!" I cried.

But their song grew louder. I was one of them and caught up in the moment. Hundreds of people streamed the packed road like water, with Romero far out of sight. The sea coalesced stronger in the march. I'd break free, but only to be grabbed by another. I was fighting a spider web of worshipers.

The sea narrowed and funneled into a building. The clangor of church bells rang above us. Large stained-glass windows stood on both sides of the entrance. They portrayed a lady in white; her eyes were closed, her palms were out, and she walked among white lilies. The crowd siphoned into the doors. My cries of protest were muffled, and my strength was sapped. The sea drained and flooded into pews.

A stone visage of the same lady stood on a stage. Another man with robes greeted the mass in front of her. Gold thread was sewn into his collar and the ends of his sleeves. Similar robes of turquoise and gold adorned others.

They pulled me into a pew with the others. My tail smacked and lashed. I struggled as best I could, but it was no use. I was trapped.

The man in front addressed the crowd. The congregation began to sing. Our hands fell to our sides.

Now's my chance.

I shuffled along the pew.

The light shone through the doorway. People stood and swayed in the aisles. The chapel stood impassable. I saw the light fade. The door started to shut. I shoved and broke through chains.

An arm pulled my shoulder. The door closed. The music stopped.

I turned, and all eyes were on me.

Two men in robes with sabers at their waists circled me.

The closer one drew his sword to my back.

"What's the meaning of this? This service ain't for your kind."

"Sorry. I was just going."

I bolted. The second guard sprang and tackled me to the ground. His elbow knocked the wind from my lungs.

"Enough!" a voice shouted from the front.

Two women in robes helped me to my feet. My back throbbed. Blood rushed to my face. My vision blurred. The speaker's voice muffled. People parted as they led me through a door further into the chapel.

&

NEXT THING I KNEW, I woke up on a bed. Light shone through a window. My back was bandaged with cloth and a woman sat beside me.

"Good evening, scaled one."

I scrambled to wrap the blanket around me as a shield. My head hit the floor as I fell out of the bed.

"My, jumpy, aren't you?"

"Where am I?"

"Safe."

That doesn't answer my question.

The woman stood up. Her robes matched the speaker's. A hood hid her face. Long brown curls bounced from inside as she paced toward the door. A wooden chair sat by the door with a robe of white.

"Our Lady Dreamer extends her apologies," she said, handing me the robe.

My eyes scanned the room. My shirt lay folded on the nightstand with a long tear through the back.

I reluctantly took the robe in my hands.

"The speaker wishes to see you."

She opened the door, ready to leave.

"Hey, you didn't answer my question. Where am I? Why did you attack me? Who is this stupid lady of yours?"

"You mustn't speak that way."

"'You mustn't speak that way,'" I mocked. "I'm not going nowhere."

She squatted down, eye level with me. Her skin appeared soft and lush. A circlet draped from her bangs with a foggy blue jewel. Her nose curled small, flat like a rabbit's. I saw her eyes. They blinked, saucer-sized and sapphire cat eyes—they were like mine.

"Do what you like. The exit's on the left. I won't stop you, but I see your heart. You're scared, afraid, and hungry. We have food, and we have answers. This world is full of darkness, my dear. I'd hate to see my healing go to waste. I see it stalks you."

"What?"

I pulled and tightened the bandages, hiding my midriff.

"A lunch is ready to the right. You're free to choose."

"Hey, wait."

The lady adjusted her hood and left without a sound.

She wasn't leaving me much of a choice. I threw on the white robe and examined myself in the mirror. The fabric was slimming and breathed like pajamas. I fixed my hair and did a double-take. My shiner —it was gone.

Who was this lady? What's after me? The thugs?

I pulled my hood up.

Time to follow the white rabbit, I suppose.

CHAPTER SEVEN

The candle sconces flickered in the hallway. The coast was clear. My heels clacked in the stone. I bit my lip and checked around me. Not a sound. I took my shoes off and tread carefully down the hall. Not a single window lit the corridor. A strand of light came from the door ajar at the end.

Many people saw me in the chapel. What if someone knows? What if word spreads? And what if this is a trap? They already seemed ready to slice me down.

The exit stood unguarded at the end of the hall.

No. I need answers. Who's "stalking" me? I need to prove my innocence. Besides, the lady healed me. She couldn't be all bad, could she?

A roaring fire lit the room in glowing orange. A red cherry table lay before me. The speaker sat at the end, tugging at a pork chop bone.

"Good. You've arrived, scaled one. Please sit," he said.

I approached the chair, surveying the table. There was a spread of various hams, lobsters, and strange meats, like roast camel and hare.

"Go on. Sit. Eat."

My eyes scanned him.

What is his angle?

"I must say, you caused quite a havoc this morning. It interrupted services entirely."

"I don't see why. I was just trying to leave."

The man stroked his chin, examining me across the table. "I see. That was a humes-only service. Yours is in the evening. Tell me, what is your name?"

His hands fell to his lap under the table.

"Kiera," I lied.

The man raised an eyebrow, intrigued.

"Interesting. Mine's Shamus."

He clapped his hands. Two men entered from both doors.

"Tell me, dear Kiera, what brings you to the temple of the Oracle?"

"The crowd swept me up. I tried to leave, but—well, you saw what happened."

"Yes, most unfortunate. Denizens are on edge, though, you must understand. This is the week of the blue moon harvest—the celebration of the Oracle's reign over Jahara and the anniversary of Aerogapolis as a nation. Even our neighboring leaders join in the parade. One last question: what do you know about the recent murders of the Wyrm Queen's Horde?"

"Not much."

He's on to me.

"Humor me."

His hand appeared white, almost as if it glowed in a pulse. I wasn't sure what to make of it.

"I know they're definitely not looking for me or you," I said, feigning a laugh.

Two men leaned over the back of my seat.

"Forgive me if I don't believe you," said Shamus.

The door opened and a force blasted the guards into the mantle. The lady in robes stood in the doorway. A purple scarf covered her face.

The man gaped at her. "High priestess! I—"

I ran to her side.

"Save it, Shamus. Leave now. You're scaring her," she said.

"She's lying. I see it in her eyes. Her heart rate quickened at every question. The mysts never lie."

"Shamus, you are relieved of duty. If I hear of just another *toe* out of line, you will be on the streets. Dismissed."

He left, muttering under his breath, and the guards soon followed.

"Thank you."

The lady only nodded. She righted my overturned chair and gestured for me to sit.

I shook my head.

"No more harm shall come to you. I'm here."

I was too shaken to eat. My mind wondered whether they had poisoned the food.

"My apologies. Shamus isn't fond of our kind."

"Our kind?"

She pulled the scarf down from her face, revealing she was the same woman from before. Her hood fell back. Two floppy brown ears draped down in her curls.

"That's much better. You're a changeling, are you not?"

"If you say so. I don't know what I am."

"Surely you can't be serious."

I sighed.

"My apologies. You poor thing. Changelings are animal folk. We are known as those of diluted humanity and sour blood from the ancients. Blessed with longer life and cursed with, well . . ."

She pushed her ears away from her face.

"If you have any more questions, let me know."

"Thank you."

"New here, I assume?" she said, chewing a biscuit from the table.

She avoided all the meats laid before us and only ate the bread.

I nodded.

"Best keep your head down, then. Changelings aren't the most well-esteemed."

"Even here?"

"Afraid so. I'm afraid I haven't much time, dear, with the festivities. Did you get enough to eat?"

"I kinda lost my appetite."

"A thousand pardons. Name's Delphi."

"So what is this place?"

"This is the temple of the Lady Oracle, the protector of Jahara, the white lily of purity and the dreamer of dreams. She watches over all to keep the spore at bay."

"Never heard of her."

"Not even the dark powers of the myst?"

"No."

"Peculiar."

"You're not going to try and hurt me, too, are you?"

"Ha. Dear sister, heavens, no. Priestesses of the white lily are to be pure and holy. That is why no one sees my face and lives, unless I allow it. No, you are safe. It is peculiar how the spores of darkness follow you, yet you have not called on it."

I cleared my throat.

"What kind of darkness?" I asked timidly.

"The spores of the myst. The dark magic, if you will. We know very little, other than it's a selfish perversion of the myst and the desires of users. As you are aware, magic is openly legal here, unlike most countries of the world, but it's still very difficult to study something so feared as the forbidden pursuits."

It made sense to me. People feared what they couldn't comprehend. They feared the unknown. I didn't really believe her, though.

I'm a good person—at least, most of the time. What evil would honestly be pursuing me?

"Earlier, you asked why the ushers attacked you?"

"Yes."

"Some of us changelings are plagued with the spore's leading."

"And they let you be in charge?"

Delphi's eyes grew wide and she cleared her throat, "My oracle has cleansed me. Many barriers remain to check and maintain my purity. My concern is with you. You know the oracle herself met a changeling of scales like yourself."

"Really?"

41

I sat on the edge of my seat. This could be our suspect.

"Yes, ten years ago. On the isle of Jahara. She had white scales with horns, like yourself."

My tail sagged. Ten years ago was too long. I began to explain my problem to Delphi.

"You wish to prove your innocence? Not an easy task, I must admit."

"Is there any way you can help me?"

"The temple is an embassy for Jahara. You are safe here if you choose to stay.

"I'd rather not," I said, thinking of Shamus.

"I understand. If not, Jahara's isles are home to many changelings. Best try there. The gates open tomorrow after the parade."

"Thank you."

"My hour has passed. I must leave you now."

"But I have more questions."

Delphi pulled up her hood and began wrapping her scarf.

"And I have a festival to attend on my lady's behalf. Come. I will see you out."

I sighed.

"You're very pretty, by the way."

Delphi remained silent. The door opened, and she beckoned me to follow.

"Why do you hide your face?"

"I'm to be her conduit. My appearance means nothing. My deeds and kindness matter."

"How can you say that? It's who you are. Why hide it?"

She put her finger to her lips and gestured for me to follow. We walked in silence down the candlelit corridor through the sanctuary to the front door.

"Good luck, and may the oracle watch over you."

I thanked Delphi and went on my way. The streets brimmed with people and burst with vibrant color. Women dressed in sunhats, silks, and fuchsia. Men wore dingy khaki, dyed cotton shirts, or leather, with long brimmed hats to manage the sun.

The market was alive. Everyone moved, snaked, and weaved in the sea of commotion and commerce. Vendors lined the street. Sales pitches were tossed and trampled under the chatter and laughter of the marketplace. Spices and sweets wafted to my nose. My stomach growled.

I must find Romero, but first things first—food.

Tents and booths with foreign fruits, grains, and vegetables extended up the market street. I also saw strange, prickly melons, and large, brown fuzzy ones, too.

Then came the sweets from the Magnificent Mister Clyde's bakery, as it would become known to me.

Mister Clyde was a peculiar man. He should have been a carny or a ringmaster, not a baker. Wiry, dark hair lay greased back past his shoulders. His goatee descended into a devilish point above a red string tie. A top hat and a thick, round paunch completed his ensemble. Mother always said, "Never trust a skinny cook."

I waited behind his current customer. His bartering gave off an air of flair. He spun his lies and pies, seemingly hypnotizing crowds into easy negotiations.

"Thank you and pleasure doing business with you. Next? Yes, how may I help a—"

The baker jumped back as if I had startled him.

"Hiya!" I said with a sheepish wave.

His skin turned pale and he grabbed his chest.

"Sorry, I didn't mean to startle you," I said. "I see you have a lot of pretty sweets back there."

The man shook his head violently before composing himself.

"Yes. Beg your pardon, my dear. We do."

"What kinds?"

"Well, my dear, nothing fancy. We have plum tarts, cherry pies, strudels . . ."

"Don't reckon I've ever had a plum before."

"Never had a plum before? A lady of the cloth? How so, my dear?"

I could never tell his character throughout the conversation. His eyes darted up and down my body and stared me deep in the eye as if he was gazing into my very soul.

"Well, I'm not actually a lady of the cloth."

"Hmm, I see."

"This is my first time in the city."

"Judging by your clothes, I suppose so. We've had very few refugees of recent. Well, on behalf of all Aerogapolis, Big Clyde bids you welcome to our fair city."

I smiled.

"Now, my dear, I will give you not one but *two* plum tarts at a bargain, since you are new, and as a grand welcome into our city. Now, you say you're new, never been here before. You sure?"

"Positive. That's very nice of you. How much?"

"Eighteen copper pieces."

"That seems a bit high for a little pie."

"You're right, my dear. Absolutely right."

He ran his hand down his pudgy, round chin, stroking his greased goatee further to a point.

"How about twelve copper pieces? They're the purest Aerogapolian plums, I assure you."

"Deal."

I gave him a fifteen and told him to keep the change as a tip. The man smiled a Cheshire grin, collecting the money.

He handed me the frosted tarts on the back of the table and I licked the frosted cat whiskers off with my fingers.

"Yes, a pleasure doing business with you, my dear."

Unbeknownst to me, I had just paid three times the value for a measly little treat..

I strolled the thoroughfare amidst stares and murmurs. Other people grabbed their children, keeping their distance as I approached. I didn't think much of it and reckoned, even in a place as big as this, there had to be somebody who hadn't seen someone like me.

I made my way down, enjoying my lunch after my long journey, trying to take in the sights as best I could. There were so many people around it was hard to see anything. It didn't help that I was only five feet tall.

The buildings sprouted up like weeds that reached toward the sun. Older buildings lacked rhyme or reason for their location, and the newer ones seemed to allow for wider streets in the market. I wouldn't learn how to tell which was which until later.

At home, buildings didn't go past two stories, the tallest being the three-story clock tower. Here in the city, they rarely stayed at one. There were five-story windmills looking over the corners of the city. The blades cast shadows down inside the city walls. As I began to walk even further into the city, I felt a hand grasp my shoulder.

I turned to see Romero scowling down at me.

"Plum tart?" I weakly grinned up at him.

CHAPTER EIGHT

The frosting smeared over my cheeks. Romero shook his head and grabbed my arm, dragging me into an alleyway. "Kid, you've got to be more careful."

"Why? What's wrong?"

"You're not skipping out on me, are you?"

My back pressed against the wall. I feigned a laugh. "Ha. Of course not."

His eyes bulged, staring me down. "Good. Otherwise, it's a knife to the gut. Understood?"

I nodded.

"Good. Where have you been and who's seen you?"

"Nobody."

He paced, giving me passing glances. "Hmm. You're a terrible liar, you know that?"

"I'm sorry."

Romero sighed. He patted me on the shoulder. "Don't sweat it, kid. We'll work on it. You had me a bit worried. You've been gone for hours."

"How'd you find me?"

Romero smirked. "I just so happen to be a master detective, among other things."

"Yeah, right."

"Don't believe me? Church bells, and you disappear. The church lets out, and you reappear. How's that sound, my dear Watson?" he said, throwing the hood of my robe back. "Only clergy of the temple and refugees gifted them wear such ceremonial clothes. Your 'humble' robe makes you a target a mile away."

"It does not," I protested. My stomach growled again. I pulled out another tartlet and stuffed my face.

"How much did you pay for that?"

"Oh, the man said it was a bargain—two for twelve." I offered him the smiling kitten tart again, slowly lifting it up to his face. He pushed it away.

"Just as I thought."

"What's that supposed to mean?"

"You stick out. You need to lie low."

"It's because I'm ugly, isn't it?"

He handed me a handkerchief to wipe my face and started to rub his chin. "No. But some clothes wouldn't hurt. Sad to say, even here your kind isn't much favored."

"Even here?"

He nodded. That had been half my reason for coming. I struggled to believe it.

"More so here than others, so I'm told. Buck up. I'll show you around. I hear the parade will begin shortly."

He held out his hand. I wiped my face and took his hand. He led me out in the square. His eyes darted toward the arch of the city gate. Two guards stood at attention on both sides, inside and out, and two circled on the tall granite wall above it.

"First, you need to get a feel for the place. Clothes will be a good start. They'll help you feel like a local."

Romero was always quick-tongued and said exactly what people wanted to hear, both of them qualities which got us into trouble. I felt there was nothing wrong with my clothes, though, besides the tear down my back.

Bartering is an interesting subject, especially in Aerogapolis. There's the "first price" and there's the real price. The first price is usually "eight" regardless of its coin denomination or whether it is worth it or not. Value is determined by what one will give up and varies from person to person.

For example, Romero took me to a man selling brightly-hued cloaks. He also had a worried look at my first approach, but then he composed himself and saw this as the business opportunity of a lifetime.

"Greetings, friends, and how may I serve you today?" He had the usual vendor look, complete with flashy suit and a red string tie, only he was thinner than most who sat all day.

"She needs a cloak," said Romero.

"Yes, and the, uh . . . lady does." The vendor seemed unsure if I was female. "And she—what lovely woman wouldn't, with her beautiful . . ." He stopped and looked me up and down. He coughed. "Right, well, you get the picture. Would the lady like a nice pink cloak?"

My heart turned downcast, my spirits crushed. That skinny tightwad couldn't find one good thing about me. Maybe if he couldn't see any good in me, no one else would either. Proving my innocence was going to be an uphill battle.

Romero turned to me and then back to the vendor. "She'll take the indigo. It'll bring out her eyes."

"Yes, sir, of course. Anything for the wonderful," he choked at the word, "*couple* here today. That'll be eight hundred."

Romero spat something back in a language I didn't understand. Then countered with, "Thirty."

"Seven hundred," the skinny man grumbled back in the same tongue.

They both shot back and forth, refusing to budge. Romero's sharp tongue dickered. The slender vendor danced until, finally, he gave up. The cloak sold at a hundred pieces—out of Romero's pocket, thank goodness. He also bought me some black leather boots, seeing as I hadn't owned my very own pair of shoes since age six, and heaven forbid I'd have to wear Angela's heels any longer. I offered to pay him back some-how, but he refused. I guess the old two-face had his moments.

Romero showed me the rest of the town. As a whole, Aerogapolis was a growing 'center of the arts.' Expansive, thriving theaters dotted the city. Vibrant murals of sunsets baked on the marble stone. Box kites hung on laundry lines from the taller houses. This had been the place of the first airship experimentation.

With the coastal breeze, the idea of flight was as genius as the town was beautiful. Plum, pomegranate, and olive trees dotted the hillside. Doves cooed from street lantern nests. Large windmills turned on the horizon, and strange, large strands of piping ran across the rooftops from building to building. I asked Romero what the windmills were for and he said it was a surprise.

Drums boomed in the distance. Guards moved the crowds along. The parade was starting. Horns blared, announcing the arrival of the entourage. A legion of soldiers marched down the street.

First, a cluster of men in petticoats, leathers and rusty metal. White sashes embroidered with a golden bell adorned their chests. This was the Aerogapolian militia.

Behind them strolled the Honorable Chief of Police, Silas Francisco, and Grand Justice Javier Cobarde, one of the evilest cowards I ever met. Justice Cobarde strode in splendor and coveted applause. He raked it in, fed on it. He posed, stroking his chin and goatee like a runway model, and blew kisses to the spectators.

Commissioner Francisco stood tall. His salt-and-pepper hair was combed over his balding scalp. Ever the man of duty, he remained stoic and vigilant, even during such festivities. He waved and nodded. No smile dared disturb his wrinkled brow.

Following them were a few new recruits and uniformed police deputies of the various forces.. I say "forces" due to the strange politics of the ownership of the pier. Ironically, they were more organized than the military. The recruits dressed in freshly polished breastplates and white sailor hats. They haphazardly marched in time. The commissioner scowled at those who failed to keep perfectly in line.

The embassy of the White Lily followed quickly behind. Some spectators booed. Others remained silent. A split became clear between silent admiration and vocal demonization. There was no sign of Delphi. Shamus led the march. It felt wrong to wear the same colors as him.

Then came the real show. Mummers, unicyclists, and clowns paraded in neon escapades and skylarked through streets. Ladies twirled and danced with elegant spins and ballet twists. Banners rose high and cannons shot confetti in celebration.

Children chased the confetti and tossed it like snow. Everyone laughed and smiled. They toasted to their country with flags in one hand and beer in the other. "Long live Aerogapolis! May good fortune smile on us all." It felt the festivities would never end.

At the back of the parade was a strange lot. A few people dared to jeer at them but were quickly silenced by police.

Men in armor, soldiers clad in cadet steel, marched next. They were one body, unified and heavily armed. The red flag of Northstrand, the republic from the south, flew high.

Behind them wheeled an elegant closed coach inlaid with gold. A silhouette of a man appeared behind the curtains.

"Who's that?"

Romero's eyes remained fixated. He didn't answer.

Behind that, a second carriage moved slower. The top was open. The dignitary's face stretched long and clean-shaven. His eyes burned like fire. In the front, his buzzed hair stood at attention and braided in the back. Some people bowed. Murmurs rose. A few guards saluted. Others did not.

"Who's that?" I asked again.

"That would be the Magistrate Stewart Vonn Beauregard, an arbiter between nations. Puppet is more like it. Here to protect the consul himself, no doubt. Let's go."

"But I want to see the rest of the parade."

Romero yanked at my arm.

"That *was* the parade."

My eyes caught the rear of the carriage and more soldiers following as he pulled me away.

"Trust me, kid, you aren't missing much. The rest is just propaganda. I say this looks like a prime opportunity. Police should be occupied for a while. It's time to get to work. Now, how about that training?"

CHAPTER NINE

"Thievery is a craft passed from generation to generation," Romero, the windbag, began. "Here we go. I'll spare you the lecture. Bottomline, keep your blade sharp and your wits sharper. If you don't have your wits, you are nothing. The world's greatest bandit can know all the tricks and have all the tools of the trade, but if he doesn't have the nerve to handle them, he's dead. Gallows. Knowledge and nerves: it's as simple as that. Improvisation is everything in the life of an escape artist like me."

He gave me a few bobby pins to practice lockpicking in my spare time. "Something basic," he called it. I'd have hated to see "difficult."

Romero rambled on about how my mind was my greatest weapon. Then it was my eyes because . . . *yadda, yadda, yadda* . . . and then he flipped again, saying my heart. We practiced a few scenarios, testing my wit for half an hour. Then the crowd dispersed and training ended. It would continue almost daily with brief lessons on manipulation, espionage, and sleight of hand.

Romero was right, I was much less noticed in my indigo cloak. I just wished I wasn't so sweaty. Most people beyond the vendors kept to themselves. As we walked the northern thoroughfare in the sunset, we saw many street performers.

Large crowds gathered to see the mummers and the musicians. The people roared in laughter and applause. They begged for more. Then there was a different one: this short, stumpy boy with suspenders and oversized white gloves who begged for a crowd.

"Please? Please, anyone? Does anybody want a laugh?"

The occasional passersby gave him a sideways glance and carried on with their business, too busy to be bothered.

"How about a fortune? I can read your fortune. Somebody? Anybody? Please?"

By now Romero had coached me, and I knew the drill: eyes straight, head down, mind your own business and they'll mind theirs. That's all there was to it. But still, I couldn't help but feel sorry for the poor kid.

"You, miss. You wanna see a trick?" He tugged on my cloak. He stared up at me with a puckered lip and took a step back at the sight of my scales.

I turned to Romero who was shaking his head.

"Sure."

Romero facepalmed.

"Oh, goodie." He began mumbling to himself, "All right, Simon, don't screw this up." He shuffled through his pockets. "All right, ma'am, pick a card, any card."

I did so.

Romero stood behind me with his arms crossed, unconvinced this was worth our time.

As I reached for a card, Simon shook his head and told me to pick another. I tried again, and he did the same. I picked the middle, and he excitedly nodded, giving me a thumbs up. I took the card and followed his instructions to hold it close and out of his sight. I looked at the card.

He closed his eyes and nervously guessed, "All right . . . seven of clubs."

I shook my head.

"Jack of diamonds."

Wrong again.

"Oh, shoot."

He tossed his hat on the ground. The card began to flutter. With the blink of an eye, it became a dove.

"Well, at least that trick worked."

Immediately, four doves flew out of his slacks and in various directions.

"Never mind," Simon sighed.

Romero stepped up behind me.

"Take note, boy, nothing good ever comes from magic."

"I thought it was splendid. I've never seen anything like it," I said.

Truly, I hadn't. This was my first time seeing magic with my own eyes. Really, it was pseudo-magic, but what did I know?

"Thanks," Simon said. "At least somebody thinks so. Aerogapolis is one of the last havens where magic is not outlawed."

"Yet," Romero was quick to note.

"Magic is a gift of the myst, and only special sorcerers like me can wield it. I'm sure someone like yourself can do much more than I can," Simon said to me.

"What do you mean by that?" I asked.

"Pay him no mind, Kiera. The boy's not even a proper magician."

"Well, miss, people like you—"

Romero interrupted, "Magic is a curse, not a gift, boy. Make no mistake about it."

"Enough. I want to hear what he has to say," I said.

Romero shook his head in disgust.

"Go on, Simon," I said.

"Well," Simon continued, "people like you are known to be incredible magicians."

"So, there are more people like me here? Where?"

The boy nodded. "Down by the docks. Mother never lets me go. She says it's too dangerous."

"You best listen to her. There's nothing but trouble there," Romero chimed in.

"Let's go," I decided.

"Kiera, didn't you hear what I said? You're racing to get your other eye bashed in down there. Besides, you'll never get in without your papers in order. We'll talk later. Preferably," he faced Simon, "someplace private."

I stood over Simon. "Anything you want to say to me, you can say in front of him."

Romero sighed. "Aerogapolian prison is not a place you wanna end up. Men of my stature wouldn't be caught dead there again. I mean, what would my fans think?"

"To heck with your 'fans,'" I said. "I need my name cleared, and a little exploring wouldn't hurt. Haven't you ever wanted to know who you are or where you came from?"

Romero shook his head. "I prefer to forget. Remember why we're here. We made a deal—you said anything, remember? You hold up your end of the bargain, and we'll see to your sightseeing . . . time permitting."

Romero wandered off into the crowd. I called out after him, but he kept walking.

I looked down at Simon and placed a copper coin in his cup.

"I enjoyed the show. Keep practicing," I told him, and raced off after Romero.

Simon waved goodbye and looked down in his little tin cup with a glowing smile on his face.

I found Romero standing with his back leaning against the wall of an inn.

"Hey, what was with you back there?"

"We'll discuss it later."

"You bullied some poor kid and won't even tell me why?"

"Yup. Don't like it? Too bad."

He turned away from me and walked into the inn.

I stormed in after him. Tables dotted the dimly lit interior. There was a bar at one end and a stage at the other. A small desk sat by the front door next to a set of wooden stairs.

"Don't you walk away when I'm talking to you," I called after Romero.

He ignored me and rang the bell on the desk. A lady with suntanned skin stood behind the counter. A red dress hugged her enormous figure where I wished it hadn't. She had shoulder length, thick, black hair, like horsehair, parted in the middle.

"Evening, Hazel," Romero said.

"Evening, darling. What can I do you for? Haven't seen you in a while."

"One room, please."

"Wrangled in another, did you?"

Romero shot her a stern look as he grabbed the key and marched upstairs.

I followed.

"Hey, do you want to tell me what that was all about or what?"

"Not really, no."

He unlocked the door and gestured with a jerk of his head for me to follow.

"All you need to know is to be careful what ideas you put into your head. Fantasies and dreams, like magic, will be the end of you."

I entered the room and he shut the door.

"What do you mean?" I asked.

He shut the curtains and searched the room for a hidden person?

"Who are you looking for?" I asked.

"No one, but you never know who's listening in. As the boy said, magic is illegal everywhere but here, and for good reason. Many a man has been led down a path of destruction seeking knowledge of the myst. Myst doesn't run as thick as it did after the war of the ancients, but it still lingers, even now in the veins of the earth."

"How do you know all this?"

Romero sighed and on the bed. He pulled a small notebook from his breast pocket.

"I've seen it with my own eyes. Magic's dangerous business, kid. Such destruction. Man isn't fit to wield such power."

"What destruction? You're not making any sense."

I stood silently as Romero thumbed through the pages of the journal. The two rings on his hand shimmered. On the back cover, written in small gold print, was, "Property of L.H."

Outside, we heard a loud whistle, then a dull crackling sound. An explosion popped, followed by another similar crackling, almost like a drum roll. I pulled open the curtains. Another pop, and then another in the atmosphere, and streams of gold ran down like a dandelion in the starry sky.

"What was that?"

Romero opened the window to the roof.

"Care to find out?" he asked.

"Don't think this means you're off the hook."

"Fireworks," Romero said.

He stepped out onto the green-shingled roof and held his hand out for me to follow. Another rocket popped and crackled in fantastic silver suns.

"Aren't they lovely?"

I turned and there were lanterns in the street brighter than I had ever seen. We sat down on the roof

"Everything is so bright. These lanterns—they're everywhere."

"Remember the windmills?"

I nodded.

"Well, those power everything without coal or oil. Fascinating, isn't it?"

I nodded again, taking in the fireworks.

"I could stay here forever," I said. "Is it like this every night, with fireworks?"

Romero laid down on the roof and began to think.

"Actually, no. You have a point there. Fireworks only occur—yes! We can work with this."

I kept asking him all night what it was, but each and every time he had the same response. He would look at me and smile and tell me I would have to wait and see. Old Green Eyes was fond of secrets and the tease.

CHAPTER TEN

I lay beside Romero on the roof most of the night. My eyes glanced over at him. I loved the way the fireworks flickered, revealing his face in the dark. He was quite handsome then—in my eyes, at least.

I scooted closer to him when he wasn't looking, reached for his hand, and extended my tail to reach over his shoulder. In the crackling and dim light, I could see the look on his face was not what I had expected. He drew his hand away and sat up.

Romero scratched the back of his head. "Look, uh, kid, I don't want you to get the wrong idea here."

"What's wrong?"

I sat up to eye-level with him.

"Kiera, you're a sweet girl and all, but let's not get carried away here. You're just a kid."

"What do you mean? What was all that with shopping today? I just thought . . . well, maybe . . . you know."

Romero sighed. "I like you and all."

I smiled, and my tail swayed a little side to side.

"But not that way. We make a great team, in this contract. But our arrangement is only for a little while."

My shoulders rose as I sighed. I stood up to leave. My tail drooped and dragged along the shingles. He called after me, but I ignored him.

As I got ready for bed, I shut the window, leaving Romero on the roof. *That will teach him to be too good for me.* I felt sick to my stomach, ashamed and stupid for thinking anyone could ever like me.

You know, the usual teenage stuff.

I woke up the next morning and . . . nothing. Gone. There was a note on the nightstand. No signs of forced entry, everything lay just as neat as when we came in. I never read the letter. Instead, I crumpled it up and tucked it away in my pocket. Who needed him? I decided I could prove my innocence by myself, and there was nothing he could do to stop me.

I got dressed and headed downstairs. Frying pans clanged and Hazel washed dirty glasses in a metal wash bin. A sizzling sound and the smell of bacon permeated the air. My stomach growled. I had gone to bed hungry. I may have been ready to go through with things on my own, but not on an empty stomach.

"Well, our desert flower emerges," Hazel called from the bin, scrubbing a mug. "I've never seen Old Slim taking a liking to your kind before."

I sat at the bar with a hand on my head.

"He didn't," I said.

Hazel dropped the mug, splashing water everywhere. One cook shot her a dirty look and cursed her in a tongue I didn't understand. A look of surprise on her face.

"Sorry to hear that."

She wiped the suds on her frilly pink apron that was two sizes too small for her grand bloatedness.

"What can I get you?"

I shrugged.

"How 'bout the special?" she asked.

I nodded. She tapped a bell on the counter and the kitchen staff stood at attention. Hazel rattled off their marching orders, and with a clap of her hands, they sprang to battle. Eggs cracked. A metal whisk swished in a glass bowl.

Hazel leaned over the bar.

"I never thought I'd see the day Old Slim turned down a pair of legs. The boy's changed," she said.

I sighed.

"Cheer up, honey. You aren't the only one. I fell for him, too."

She placed the special before me. Sunny side up eggs and bacon, shaped in a smiley face, stared at me atop a biscuit—and more eggs, scrambled. It was more food than I'd ever seen on one plate.

I stared up at Hazel with full attention.

"I was young. He went by Christopher back then. He promised me the world. Took me on an airship. Oh yes, it was wonderful. Then he ruffled me up and dumped me here."

"What'd you do?"

"Well, I picked myself up and kept going. I'll live."

She chuckled as she slapped her jiggling stomach.

"I moved on. It's not easy to hear, I know. Time passed. My work started here and now I own the place. You just need to find the right fella, and," she moved closer and whispered, "it's not *him*."

"Thanks."

"Don't mention it."

I reached into my purse to pay. She shook her head.

"Ol' Slim paid for you. He said you'd need it."

I felt even less sure how to feel.

Hazel said if I ever needed anything to let her know. I asked her to point me in the direction of the docks. It was time to play private eye.

On my way, I stopped by Big Clyde's stall for some more delicious plum tarts. To prove just how much I didn't need Romero, I tried to haggle my way. Clyde was more than happy to negotiate a lower price. I ended up saving two pieces more than last time, even after he threw in a basket. Somehow, this proved I was better off.

As I turned around with my excessive amount of pastries in a basket, I crashed into someone. I stooped down and gathered my pies. He bent down to help. My eyes darted up and I could hardly believe what I saw.

A silver breastplate gleamed, freshly polished to a bright shine. The crest sewn into his sash made it very clear he was police. His face blazed with a thick chocolate mane of fur. From it extended two pointed ears and a snout. He had the face of a German Shepherd crossed with a Siberian Husky.

The man apologized repeatedly. His voice was rough and warm, like an itchy sweater. Under his cherry beret, his crooked ear flicked in its goofy fashion. Over his badge, sewn in bold white letters was, "RECRUIT."

He handed me back my few smashed tins. I stepped back in awe, both of a cop and such a strange creature.

"You sure do like pie," he said.

I nodded. My fingers gently pried the tiny tins away from him.

His nose flicked. "Blueberry, cherry . . . plum?"

"Precisely."

I began running over my options, but all I could think to do was run.

"I don't reckon I've seen a girl with scales before."

"I could say the same of you."

My eyes scanned for the nearest alley. There were too many people. I was trapped.

"Say, are you a local?"

I feigned a laugh.

"Ha, yeah, lived here all my life," I lied.

"Great. I'm actually new in town and was hoping someone could show me around. Do you mind?"

My heavens, what have I said?

I fumbled. "Well, I don't know. I'm not the best with directions."

"Nonsense. You've lived here all your life."

"I might get you lost."

"I'm already lost. Getting lost with you doesn't sound too bad. We can be lost together. You have really pretty eyes, Miss . . . um . . ."

"Kiera. Kiera Estaban."

Came on a bit strong for my taste, but he was very sweet. I couldn't remember the last time I had received a compliment.

"Well, I'm Maxwell, but you can call me Max. You don't have to if you're uncomfortable. It's just . . ."

His ears tucked back, and he dug a small divot with his foot.

"This is my first day here. I want to be part of the sky city police someday, and like I said, I'm already hopelessly lost, and alone. I missed my peers at the parade yesterday. I'm by myself and I could use some company. But if you don't want to, that's fine, I guess."

His sad dog eyes focused on the hole his shoe had dug, then slowly looked up at me with a long face. He gazed at me with mismatched eyes, one aqua and one almond.

I bit my bottom lip and started thinking. It was hard to say no.

"Well, I have to say—"

"I knew it. Sorry to bother you."

The dog sighed, kicked a rock, and started walking. My heart went out to the poor thing, even if he smelled a little funny.

I considered it more. *Well, he certainly wouldn't be searching to bring me in if he's only been here today. He might even make the perfect cover.*

I grabbed my basket and ran after him, calling out, "Max, wait."

He turned around, looking confused.

"I'd be delighted," I said as I took his arm.

He wagged his tail and smiled at me as we went on our merry way.

Just like that, I had traded one mistake for another. That's the story of how I met my most loyal lapse in judgment. Wherever you are, Max, I'm sorry. I really am. But I'm getting ahead of myself.

CHAPTER ELEVEN

I wasn't sure how to fake a sense of direction, since I was supposed to be a 'local.' I didn't have a city map and had no idea where I was, so how was I supposed to lead Max around?

Aerogapolis was divided into eight districts and surrounded by two walls—for protection in the highly unlikely event of a siege.

How was I supposed to get to the docks with my watchdog in tow and prove my innocence? Of course, this would mean I couldn't say I did it all by myself. But at least I'd have the joy of rubbing it in Romero's grubby face.

Max and I walked arm-in-arm. He remained silent. His ears raised and turned. His nose flicked, taking in the smells. He seemed content just being along for the ride wherever we went.

As we reached the Southtown district, the foot traffic slackened in the streets. The houses stood in rows, nearly touching each other. Broken glass littered the sidewalk. As we walked along a yellow ribbon blew outside the barbershop. Bingo. This definitely had to be the scene of one of the latest crimes. The docks could wait.

Time to practice my storytelling.

"Uh, Max, this is the Danzinger Barbershop," I said, reading the sign. "Do you mind if I stop in right quick?"

Max turned his head, looking at me funny, but agreed to hold my basket at the stoop.

Time to get work. I'm going to prove Romero wrong.

Inside, people lined the benches on the walls. Eight chairs spun with the snipping of scissors and the slurping of shaving cream. At the counter, a clerk was being interviewed by a police officer. Grizzly men and poor families alike waited for their turn in the chair. They leaned in, eavesdropping on the interview.

"Now, you are sure you saw this, correct?" he asked, holding up a sketch.

"No, it was dark. It had scales and horns. I'm sure of it."

I found a space on a nearby bench and listened in, pulling up my hood to blend in better.

"One last time, which direction did you see the suspect flee?"

The clerk twitched as he thought. He checked over his shoulder as if being watched. "Down Seafarer's way. Toward the docks."

The officer's pencil scratched.

Bingo. Now I really have to go to the docks.

The officer continued, "Right. With any luck, we'll catch him before he leaves port. One more thing, did Peterson have any enemies?"

The clerk shook his head as he spoke. "Not that I know of. He was a good man; had trouble with the law once, but he's changed I tell you."

The officer nodded. "Right. My notes mention gang activity. What can you tell me about that?"

"He got in with the wrong crowd, I tell you. Some group called the Wyrm Queen's Horde. They took him in."

Three men walked in and passed the officer to the back room. I immediately recognized one as the man who had choked Angela, from the bar. I thought all the men from the bar had been murdered. *Now's my chance for some answers.* I rose to my feet to follow them.

The clerk appeared not to notice me, his face awkwardly flat. A pair of round spectacles hung from the bridge of his nose.

The back of the shop was poorly lit. Two or three windows provided the only real light source. The men moved steadily down the narrow hallway. They chatted amongst themselves, drowning out my footsteps.

I hugged the wall as they turned the corner. My heart raced. What was I doing? This was stupid. Why was I doing this? I took a deep breath.

It will all be worth it once I get this lead. I must prove I'm innocent.

I rounded the corner and they were gone. The room was cramped with crates piled high around a cabinet in the corner. This was bad. How could I lose them when I had them cornered? I began inspecting the crates. They were nailed shut with no way of prying them open. I opened the cabinet. Cans of shaving cream lined the top shelves. The rest lay bare. My knuckles knocked on the back. It seemed solid.

I shut the door and turned to leave empty-handed. Inches away, a large man stood over me. Tattoos lined his sleeves. His nostrils huffed hot air in my face.

I weakly waved.

He grabbed me by the shoulders and pushed me up against the cabinet.

"What are you doing here?"

"I . . . I got lost. I j—just was looking for the little girls' room."

I cringed. *Please don't bash my face in. Please don't bash my face in.*

"Go back down the hall the way you came. Ask Kyle at the counter for the key. If I catch you stealing my stock, you'll be sorry. Now get."

"Oh, bless you."

I scrambled down the hall and raced to the bathroom, true to my word, because now I needed it. My lungs squeezed. I hyperventilated. My breaths echoed off the walls.

Holy crap. I'm alive.

I couldn't believe it. My feet practically didn't touch the ground as I raced out of the bathroom, out of the shop, and yanked Max off the stoop. There was no looking back. Max moved as slow as dead weight. I pulled him by the arm into the nearest alley. Adrenaline pumped in my veins.

"What's going on?"

I shushed him.

"But I—"

I clamped his mouth shut and pressed a finger to his lips. My head peered around the corner. Denizens strolled up and down the street. Nobody followed us.

I released his snout.

"Okay, we're good."

"What happened? I thought you were just going to say hello to a friend. You were gone for half an hour."

I slid down the wall with my hands on my knees. I had to catch my breath. "I'm sorry. There was this guy and he had me cornered and,"

"Are you okay?"

I nodded.

"What happened?"

"I was in the back room and—"

"What were you doing in the back room?"

"We—I—"

I stopped. I wasn't sure what to tell him. He was still a cop, recruit or not.

"Trespassing is against the law, Kiera."

"Yes, I know, but I needed to know something."

He crossed his arms. "Which is?"

"There was a murder here a day ago. I wanted to see the place for myself."

"It's the police's job to solve crimes, Kiera."

"Yeah, but the police don't know what they're doing," I snapped.

"We do the best we can. Our job is to help people. You breaking into a place of business is not helping anyone."

"I'm sorry."

"You're okay, right? Nobody hurt you or anything?"

"No."

"Good." I focused on his badge. Maybe traveling with a cop wasn't such a good idea. "You're not going to tell on me, are you?"

Max stood over me with his arms crossed. He sighed. "I guess not," he whispered.

"Great!" I shot up and hugged him. "I'll make it up to you, somehow."

Max's stomach growled.

"I still got some strudels if you're hungry," I said.

He smiled and added, "Okay, I forgive you."

We strolled a few blocks to find a place to sit. I was eager to leave Southtown. Max didn't ask many more questions on the way. All he wanted to confirm was that I was okay. He took my arm again as we walked. His palms gripped gently, yet firmly. His fingers were padded like hybrid paws.

Soon, the row houses became storefronts. The atmosphere changed here. The air ran warmer. The colors returned. Milk chocolate skinned women strode in vibrant sundresses. The stone turned from white and brown to burnt red and tangerine murals.

Down the street, buildings parted and backed up to a large marble structure. Columns with stone lions perched, guarding two raised stair-cases divided by a fountain. It looked as good a place as any to sit and eat.

I cracked open the basket and we took in the city and strangers passing by.

A building at the top of the stairs had impressive bay windows and a large dome with chiseled ivy cresting the roof.

"What's that building there?" I asked.

"You tell me." Max shrugged. "You're the travel guide."

A large sign directed traffic inside, "Free festival maps and itineraries available here."

I pointed it out to him, and this became our next stop. *Maybe this could be my chance to ditch the dingbat.*

It's not that I hated having Max around or anything. A map would help both of us and he wouldn't need me anymore. I'd have less heat traveling solo. I could get to the docks and he could learn his way around the city. It would be a shame to see him go. He was an idiot—charming, but still an idiot.

After lunch, we climbed the stairs and entered the building. A mural of pink clouds, birds, and serpents with angel wings decorated the hundred-foot ceilings.

Dark hardwood covered the floors, tables, benches, and service desk.

The footsteps and voices of visitors reverberated off walls and vaulted ceilings.

A man greeted us. His button-down uniform stiffened in navy blue. A golden pin of a phoenix rising from the pages of a book adorned his cap. I recognized him as an Alexandrian Bookkeeper, a watchman of the world's libraries.

"Afternoon. What may I do you for?"

His face soon turned to disgust at the sight of me.

"We saw your sign for maps."

"Ah, yes, another tourist. My heavens, they're multiplying," he grumbled. "Right this way."

The hardwood turned to a tile floor in checkered black and white. I couldn't help but think I'd been here before.

"First time in the city, I suppose?"

"Yes," Max answered.

"Well, welcome to one of the greatest treasure troves of knowledge you'll ever see."

"The Prometheus's Library," I interjected.

"Correct."

"It has been one of my dreams from childhood to see it in person."

"Never thought I would hear that from your kind."

"Really?"

"That was sarcasm."

"I thought books were forbidden?" asked Max.

"They are," I said.

The bar hop butted in, "Only those approved by the governing bodies for study and medicinal practice, and outside Alexandria. Those have been the rules since the founding of nations. You'll find Aerogapolis is much less—how shall I put it? Um, narrow-minded."

Max's head turned, not fully understanding all that was spoken. He couldn't read, anyway.

We were led toward a desk. Behind it sat a lady, reading. Her face was that of a doe, with her hair pulled into a neat bun. A deep jade pendant hung around her neck. Round rimmed glasses sat at the end of her nose.

The bookkeeper stopped a few yards away and put his arm over Max's shoulder.

"You see that there?"

Max nodded.

"That's who you gotta talk to. Good luck, boy. I envy your courage."

"What do you mean?"

"You mean you don't know?"

Max shook his head.

"Behind that counter is one of the most ferocious, beastly creatures you'll ever meet."

"Really?" Max shook a little as he spoke.

The lady's ears shot up and she glared our way.

"Shh. Not so loud. She'll hear you."

The lady scowled, shook her head, and returned to her book.

"Don't listen to him, Max," I said. "He's pulling your chain. She's just a librarian."

"Don't let appearances fool you. That one's a deadly pit viper. A witchy woman, a d—"

The lady called from the desk without looking up from her book, "You know I can hear you."

I remember thinking to myself, *A what? Ditz? Dunce? Devil?*

"I best get moving. Your map's with her. Best of luck to you, son." The bookkeeper clapped Max on his backside and Max yelped.

"You, too, sweet cheeks," he said as he did the same to me.

"Hey!"

The bookkeeper darted down the hall, snickering.

"That was uncalled for," Max growled as he glared at the exit.

"Leave him. He's not worth our time."

"But he—"

"I'll live. Let's get your map. I'm not going to let some creep tell me what to do."

I don't need Max's "protection." I'm tough and can handle myself.

Ha, who was I kidding? I was twig and a shrimp. I just didn't need the heat on my tail. Still, Max didn't own me or whatever. Unless, even back then he . . . never mind.

We stepped forward to ring the bell on the counter. The Librarian looked up at us with a raised eyebrow.

"Yes? Oh, goody," she said as she clapped her hands together and rose from her chair. She took a deep breath. "I'm so glad he didn't drive you away. You know, I was half worried he would. Minerva Teslafaughn at your service: chief librarian, administrative assistant, and head of the book club. But enough about me; let's talk about you. What can I do you for? And you, sir?"

She leaned over the counter. Her long lashes flicked in Max's face. He whimpered.

"You can call me Minnie. And how may I help a handsome stud like you?"

She turned to me.

"Why, he's so cute I could just eat him right up."

Max cowered back with his tail shaking between his legs.

"Oh my, I must have frightened the poor thing. You have nothing to fear. Nigel's just bored and spiteful, that's all. I'm not half as mean or loud or—"

Another bookkeeper shushed her as he passed by. Her glare spoke volumes. Once his back was turned, she stuck her tongue out at him.

"Anyways, what was I saying?"

"You were reassuring Max," I said.

"Yes, Maxwell, what a lovely name. And who might be better suited for you than this gorgeous desert rose? And who might you be?"

"Kiera."

She leaned into a whisper, "Rest assured, dear, he's all yours. He's much too young for a spry hen the likes of me."

"What? Him?"

"And what can I do for you two lovebirds?"

"Well, first of all, we're not—"

"Marriage planning? Aisle 234," she interrupted.

"Well, I don't—"

"Romance? Section 17 dash B."

"No. I'm trying to tell you that—"

"Erotica, perhaps?"

"What? No!"

"Max, you sly dog, you've wrangled yourself a prickly peach."

My jaw dropped. "I just met him this morning."

She pressed hands over her heart.

"Aw, love at first sight. How sweet. Come now to the secluded section 69."

My blood boiled.

I was flabbergasted how someone could be so self-absorbed and irritating.

She jumped onto a book cart and rode it like a shopping cart. "Away!"

Several bookkeepers trailed in desperate pursuit to regain some semblance of order over her.

Max limply raised his eyes from the floor, just as uncomfortable as I was. He scratched the back of his head. I rubbed my forearm, unsure how to break the ice with him.

"I think I can do without a map," he said.

"Man up. They should be at the desk. Let's just take one and go. The bookkeeper was right, anyone who talks that much is obviously demonic. I couldn't get a single word in. You see that?"

Max remained a whimpering statue. "I thought deer were shy."

Must I do everything myself?. I leaned over the desk. Nothing but books and apple cores lay on the other side, and not a single map in sight. She had to have them on her person, or they were out. That figured.

This led me to two options: either we played Minerva's games, or we made do on our own without a map. She was annoying and infuriating. On the other hand, it was past noon, and I still had to get my bearings in this new and strange place. Max seemed fine with being lost and was frankly too stupid to care. It was Romero I worried about. I needed to prove him wrong. If I went back to Hazel's at the end of the day with nothing to show for it, I'd look like an idiot, or worse, take a knife to the gut.

Aisle 69 it was, then.

"Come on, Max."

I followed the trail of skid marks.

"Hey, where are you going? Kiera? Wait up." Max hurried to catch up with me.

For a librarian, Minerva's motor skills were incredible. A few loose books littered the floors, scuff marks chalked the narrow paths, and for all this, she only hit one pedestrian. It could have been much worse.

When we finally caught up with her, she was arguing with several bookkeepers about her actions.

"Minerva, this is inexcusable," grumbled one.

"No one was hurt. It was all in good fun," she defended.

One limping bookkeeper joined the others and chimed in, "My foot begs to differ."

As we approached, we could see the overturned cart and a toppled shelf had narrowly missed another, which would have caused a domino effect.

Scratch what I said about her driving.

Their arguing intensified. Minerva waved her arms to try to calm herself down.

"Right, and I hear you, but what I'm saying is, given the choice to do it all over again, I would."

"But you're not, I hope," a bookkeeper said.

"Of course not."

The gathering breathed a momentary sigh of relief.

"It's not a party until you get all four wheels off the ground. You should try it." Minerva laughed.

The bookkeepers, in their pompous, flowing robes and formal suits, nearly pulled their hair out.

"Never in a library," they admonished.

She gave them hell. I almost felt sorry for them.

I cleared my throat. The crowd turned to see me and slowly dispersed.

"There you are," Minerva said. "Not flaking out on me now, are ya?"

"No, not at all. It was some show."

"Wasn't it, though?"

She pulled her crossed fingers from behind her back and waved them at me.

"Just wait till I find that missing wheel. That baby will be gliding again in no time. Now, about that book."

"Yes, well, you see—"

"*Flights of Fancy* was it?"

"Well, Minerva—"

"Ooh, this one is one of my favorites. Very steamy. Don't let your man catch you reading this one. Say, where is that handsome chap of yours?"

Max eased his head around the corner to check if the coast was clear of the frightening doe.

"There you are, you rapscallion, you."

Immediately, his head zipped back around the corner.

Minerva's heels clicked and caught him before he could bolt.

"Don't be shy."

Max froze and whined.

"Look—ooh, these cheeks."

She pulled his jowls into a smile.

"Minerva," I said.

"Oh, I could take you home. Momma would love you. She'd just drool all over ya," Minerva said with a giggle.

"Minerva!"

"What is it, honey?"

"We need a map. We were told you have them."

"A map? Why didn't you say so to begin with, silly goose? Now, that would be this way. Follow me."

"Minerva. Minerva, wait."

But before I could get another word in, she was gone.

Max stood motionless, then whispered, "I feel dirty."

"Come on, Max. Let's go."

Minerva gave us the grand tour of the reference section to maps of the world, nations, sewers, and history of the city. Finally, she took a breath.

"Any questions?"

"We heard you have free maps of the city."

She pulled two pamphlets from her skirt pocket.

"These?"

I snatched them from her fingers.

"Hey, that wasn't very nice. I had a grand story about how we received them. The cartographer's in prison now, and—"

"Minerva, I don't want to hear it."

"Hmph." She crossed her arms in a huff. "Well, I never."

I handed Max his map.

"Well! Well, you could have just asked for them. There was simply no need to yank them out of my hand. I mean, back in my day, we—"

"Look, even now you won't let me get a word in," I said.

Her ears tucked back. She raised her finger as if she was going to say something but thought better of it. She rubbed her chin and sighed. "I'm sorry," she offered.

I shook my head and grabbed Max by the arm to leave while we still could.

"Sorry. I don't have many friends. Here in the library talking is kind of," she faintly chuckled, "frowned upon. Let me make it up to you. It's time for my evening cup of tea. Let us unwind over some cookies and crumpets. You're right. You should have your turn to speak."

I kept walking.

"Kiera?" Max whined. His stomach growled.

"I have food in the basket," I reminded him.

"Still . . . we hurt her. It's the duty of every policeman to make every wrong right."

"You're unbelievable. *Now* you want to be around her? Let's just take what we have and go."

"Kiera."

He pointed to the overturned books and shelves the bookkeepers were trying to repair, and then at the street patrols out the window searching for the murder suspect. One had a poorly drawn sketch of a scaled figure with horns and a tail.

"I'm sure she can tell us all about the docks."

"That I can," she called from afar.

I forgot she could still hear us. "Okay, fine."

"Oh, goody," said Minerva, clapping with glee.

"Only because I'm hungry, too," I lied.

CHAPTER TWELVE

Minerva led us to a back room underneath a stairwell.
"I must say, I'm quite dry. Parched, even. Totally parched. Why, if I were a flower—and most ways I am—I'd wilt. You'll catch me if I faint, won't you, Maxy?"

I swear her lips never stopped flapping.

"Here we are."

She opened the door into a wide, candlelit room. It was cozy and snug.

"Now, these lights run on windmill power. Aren't they just swell?"

There was a large golden loveseat in front of a coffee table and a rocking chair, and all around us were books. Books everywhere. They covered the walls to the ceiling. The shelves stopped at a hall tree by the door and stretched to another closed door.

All the décor had a garden theme. Apple knickknacks. Apples in the fruit bowl. Weeds and ivy were carved into the baseboards, and the fruit bowl itself was held aloft on the backs of four golden dragons as legs.

"Welcome to my lair," Minerva said with a giggle. "I'm going to put a kettle on. Make yourselves at home. You two try to behave now."

I whispered to Max, "There's still time to leave. Now's our chance."

Max shook his head and sat on the couch. "That would be rude," he said.

I groaned and sat beside him with my legs and arms crossed. "You don't like her, do you?" I asked.

He shook his head. "Why? Are you jealous?"

"Of course not. We're nothing, but you try telling *her* that."

His head hung a tad lower. "We're nothing? Not even friends?"

"I hardly know you. Let's say 'acquaintances.'"

Max nodded in silence. His thumbs twiddled with his map in his lap.

"Come and get it," Minerva exclaimed with a tray of cookies and tea.

Max approached the cookies with caution.

"Don't worry. They're raisin, not chocolate. You really didn't think I'd poison them, did you?"

Yes.

Max nibbled off a corner. His eyes widened. He began gorging himself on the tray.

"I'd say somebody has a sweet tooth."

She passed the saucers. I begrudgingly took mine. Minerva brought her cup to her lips, blew, and lapped like a dog. Max followed suit.

I had never attended a tea party before. Growing up, I was much more of a mud pie kind of gal. Regardless, I wasn't doing that.

Minerva laughed. "Come, now, Kiera. Relax. Kick off your shoes. Let your hair down. Get wild, natural, and frisky." She shook her hair out and put her bare feet on the coffee table for emphasis.

"I'm fine," I assured her.

She rolled her eyes.

"You're no fun. Do tell, what species of changeling are you, Kiera?"

I shrugged.

"Hmm, interesting. I'd like to think of myself as an avid reader, and I think I can read you two pretty well."

This ought to be good. She can't even tell we aren't a couple.

"Shoot," I snickered, sipping my tea. The hot liquid warmed my insides going down.

"Max," she began, "you are loyal to a 'T.' You have a heart bigger than your stomach."

76

Max nodded with his cheeks full and crumbs falling from his snout. We all laughed.

"Kiera, you're harder to read. I don't like the name Kiera. You need to loosen a bit. How 'bout a nickname. 'Kiki,' all right?"

Max laughed. "I like it. Kiki sounds cute."

I shook my head.

"We'll put a pin in it," Minerva said. "Kiera, you're guarded. I can tell by the glow in your eyes that you adore books as much as I do. You're strong-willed, yet weaker than you'd let others believe, and you hate to admit it. You're determined, worried, and anxious. Something's been troubling you since you've arrived. Now tell me . . . how'd I do?"

I shook my head, denying it.

The cuckoo clock chimed on the wall.

"Oh, it's two o'clock!" Minerva exclaimed. "No wonder I'm exhausted."

Max sprang to his feet and yelled, "Two! I'm late!" He licked his paws, combed his hair, and brushed away the broken cookie bits. "I can't be late. I'm so going to be demoted."

"Max, are you all right?" I asked.

He began hyperventilating.

I rushed beside him. "It's okay. Breathe. Just breathe and tell us what's wrong."

"I'm late."

"Okay, late for what?"

"Inspection. That's why I needed directions. I don't know the way to the barracks."

Minerva began unfolding the map. "Relax." she said. "You didn't know your way. Now you do. Look, sweetheart, you're here, and the barracks are here. See? Straight line. Can't miss it."

Max nodded.

I poured him another drink.

He spilled half on the floor as he sloppily lapped it up.

"Better?"

He nodded. "Thank you. I really must be going now."

"So soon?" Minerva said with a frown.

"Afraid so. It was nice meeting you." Max turned to me and said, "I hope we cross paths again someday, acquaintance."

"That came out wrong," I tried to explain. I pulled his arm back as he turned to leave. "I'm sorry. Friends?" I extended my hand for him to shake.

He looked down at my hand and pushed it away. His arms squeezed me tight. I almost squealed in surprise.

"Friends," he agreed.

I awkwardly tensed and pushed him away.

He scratched the back of his head. "Right. I, uh, better be going."

"You still have crumbs all over your face."

"Really?"

I laughed. "Yep, hold still."

"Stop. I got to go."

"It will just take a second." I licked my thumb and wiped the bits away from his face. His warm breath brushed across my cheek as he leaned in close. His black button nose glistened wet. His eyes were like saucers and reflected mine back in them, unblinking. I licked my thumb again, combed his whiskers, and made moist crosses against his lips and petite chin.

Minerva knelt in behind us, whispering, "Kiss her."

We both leapt back ten feet. Minerva cackled.

"Nope. Friends. Just friends, okay?"

"Okay. I, uh—"

"Yeah, you better go. I—"

He scratched his head and I held my arm behind my back.

"See you around, then?" he said with a nervous laugh.

"I'll be staying at Hazel's Inn if you want to visit."

He nodded.

"My chambers are always open to you, too," Minerva teased.

"Right. Leaving. Going now. Bye." Max bolted.

Minerva called after him, "What, no kiss? She got a hug. I want a wet one, sugar lips."

The door slammed. His footsteps thumped as he sprinted as fast as he could.

"Pity," Minerva said, sipping her tea.

It was then I realized he'd left me alone with the deer. I turned to see her checking her pocket watch.

"What's the big idea?"

"Whatever do you mean, child? Come. Sit. Have more tea and unwind. The evening's still young."

"Can't you see you how uncomfortable you were making him?"

"Yes. It's quite fun, actually. But why should you care? 'Acquaintances,' wasn't it? Come, sit, drink a bit more."

"That's sick."

"Sick? Sweet pea, you've got me all wrong. He reads like an open book, can't you tell?"

She poured me another cup and gestured for me to sit down.

I groaned and sat back on the loveseat alone.

"Let me give you some advice, girl to girl, but you got to hear me out first, okay?"

"Yeah, sure, whatever. Just get to why you were torturing him."

"That bad, huh? No, I'll hear no more of it. Surely you must know what it's like to be called a monster."

That I did.

"Kiera, changelings—people like us—are few and far between. Many hate us for no reason, and some with good reason, and if you can find the right one, take him."

"What are you saying?"

Minerva laughed to herself, then said,

"You still don't get it? He likes you. Max likes you. Smitten."

"What? No, we're just friends. We just met this morning."

"And I'm telling you he's free-fallen head over heels."

"So why were you leading him on?"

"Two reasons—mainly to spare him the heartache. Look at those eyes of his. Umm, adorable. Maybe cheer him up, even. Look at you. You're clearly avoiding or using him."

"I am not. What's your other reason, then, Miss Matchmaker?" I mocked.

"Easy. It's just fun to mess with people. Did you see the look on the faces of those pompous pricks upstairs? Priceless."

The basement room felt chilly. I took another sip of the warm tea. There was a strange hint of something I hadn't caught before.

"You're terrible."

"Come now. Lighten up. Loosen up a bit. It's just us girls now, so spill your guts. What's your story?"

"Was that your plan? To get rid of Max?"

"So, I'm a monster now, am I? Just some carnivorous animal out to kill and destroy and not care who gets in my way?"

I stared down into my cup.

The clock ticked in the silence between us.

"That's all we are to humes, aren't we?"

"Humes?"

"Humans."

I nodded.

"I must say, it's brave—mighty brave—of you to wear your scales more publicly than I have."

"Thank you," I said and sipped my tea again. It burned going down.

"What's it like?" she asked.

"Beg your pardon?"

"I hide here with my treasure trove of books away from the outside world. When it comes down to it, though, humanity is the real treasure. I've read a quarter of this library and still can't understand people and why we do the things we do. I've seen many a lifetime come and go. Would you know I'm two hundred years old?"

She floored me. There wasn't a wrinkle or feeble bone in her body. She was thin in frame, yes, but not shrunken, hunched, or anything.

"You don't look a day over thirty."

"Why, thank you, dear. That means my treatments are working."

"Is that normal for us?"

"You mean you don't know?"

I shook my head. *Apparently, I don't know anything compared to anyone.*

"If I knew, would I be asking?"

"Fair enough. Changelings are known to live a bit longer than humes, provided you can survive the onslaught of prejudice and persecution. A hundred is average, but that depends on the species, mind you. You said you didn't recognize your species?"

"I didn't even know my race until recently."

"Come. Follow me."

The lady sounded like a broken record.

She stood up and led me to the room behind her.

My legs felt wobbly and the blood rushed to my head. I just assumed I'd been sitting funny.

Inside the room, a well-made bed stood in the corner beside a chest of drawers. Shelves, with various bottled liquids, lined the walls. A small chimney stood across from the bed with many figures of large, winged creatures with scales. In the center of the mantle on a stand was a single golden plate, curved in an oval and sharp around the edge.

She handed it to me.

"Careful now, don't drop it."

The sides of the plate cut my palms. It weighed at least five pounds.

"Do you know what this is?"

"Heavy."

She smirked. "True. But do you know where it came from?"

My vision blurred a little. I glanced at the dolls and back at the plate. "A dragon?"

"Close enough. A humming drake. But, yes, sadly they are indistinguishable from dragons. I think this may be your species."

"How so?"

"Your scales shine like this. It's unmistakable."

My stomach gargled. I belched.

"I say, Kiera, are you all right?"

I dropped to my knees as I felt a stabbing pain in my gut.

Minerva pulled out her watch and stopped it.

"I must say, your constitution is impeccable. Only more to build my case of lineage."

"What did you do to me?"

"Nothing, dearie. I thought my cup of tea felt weak, and you've proved my suspicions correct."

She sipped from her cup again.

"Blech. Needs more mother's milk."

She pulled a small glass bottle of brandy from her bra and poured it in her cup.

"Hey, airhead, what did you do to me?"

"Now, it's not nice to call other names. In fact, you should be thanking me. You drank my medicine, that's all."

"Thank you?"

"You're welcome. If anything, it would've only loosened your tongue, that's all. Open up to Max."

I felt lightheaded and the room was very cold.

"Let me find an antidote and I'll have you patched up in a jiffy. On the bright side, we can spend more time together."

I groaned.

"Hang in there, dearie. Lighten up." She thumbed through the bottles. She hummed and sang a song.

> *The moon was shining sulkily*
> *Because she thought the sun*
> *Had got no business to be there*
> *After the day was done—*
> *'It's very rude of him,' she said,*
> *'To come and spoil the fun.'*

"Here it is! Charcoal. Lighten up. You're fine. Smile. I know there's a fun side in there. Let it out."

I vomited. The drugs made the fluid appear as an iridescent rainbow puddle.

"That's the spirit. Speaking of spirits . . ."

Besides another bottle of brandy, Minerva handed me the jar of charcoal tablets and walked over to the chimney. Her nose flicked, sniffing the pot of tea over the fire.

"Heavens, you may need a doctor. This brew is positively potent with brandy, and my beauty medicine probably didn't help."

You think?

Minerva helped me into a chair by the nightstand.

The clock chimed.

"Three o'clock," Minerva observed. "I wonder how Max is doing. Oh no, Max. The tea!"

She scrambled to the looking glass over the vanity. Myst rose from the ground around her. The reflection of the worried librarian began to wrinkle and ripple, and then it was replaced with an image of a pier overlooking the beach.

Within the image, Max stood at attention, saluting. His tongue stuck out from the corner of his mouth.

"Oh, thank goodness he's all right."

The visage faded in the mirror.

"How did you do that?" I asked.

"This old thing? It's a looking glass, dear. Powerful magic, lots of sweat, and training. Why? Wanna spy on the precious pooch some more, eh?"

"No. I told you, if anything, we're just friends."

"Well, I *do*."

Her chest rose and fell as she breathed. Myst accumulated in the room like steam. The picture fizzed and warbled. "Darn water interfering again."

"Good."

"Suppose it's for the best. He's much too young for me."

"How's it work?"

"That's the fun of it. I'm not entirely sure. Mysts are a fickle mistress. Here's what I do know: it'll only show you the area around a person you have seen or are familiar with, and you can't scry where there's no myst —like over water. There are other quirks that come and go, of course. It's very taxing magic."

I wondered if it could see through walls. It would've been very useful at the barbershop. Maybe, if I couldn't see where they went, I could see where the men were now. I needed a better lead on the murderer and who framed me.

"Can you show me?"

"Ooh, the shrinking violet's a tiger lily in disguise after all."

I laughed.

"I may," she continued. "But on one condition: are we friends? Can you forgive me for the whole tea thing? Please don't leave."

I belched—feeling a small relief in my distressed stomach. My vision steadied. I nodded.

"Are the tablets at least helping?"

"Yes, thank you, Minerva."

"Enough with 'Minerva' this and 'Minerva' that. I won't hear any more of it. Call me Minnie."

"Thank you . . . Minnie."

She squeezed me tighter than she should've. I felt ready to hurl again.

The librarian babbled away about the inner mechanics of the mirror and how she had smuggled it here.

Truth be told, I didn't care. I couldn't have cared less. But seeing her eyes lit up in her devilish grin and hearing her senile cackle made me feel better. It took my mind off the pain at least. Minnie was all right . . . sometimes.

CHAPTER THIRTEEN

"So, tell me about this man of yours. What does he look like?" Minerva asked me.

"Let's see . . . he's tall, muscular, tribal tattoos, rich chocolate skin . . . ," I thought aloud.

"Yes, go on. Tall, dark and handsome. Ooh-la-la, our lady does have a wild side! Tell me more so I can—what am I saying? You've got the spark in you, right?"

"The what?"

"Of course you do. Don't be shy. Visualize him in your head and put your hands on the glass. I'll do the pedals, you just steer."

Minerva's magic looking glass pressed like ice against my fingers.

Myst began pouring into the room. An unsettling sensation came over me and I couldn't tell if this was real or a dream. It could have been the mysts or the drugs. Probably the drugs. The hoodlum from the barbershop, the one who'd escaped, stood before me in the mirror. I leaned in and tapped on the glass. From where I had seen the man, the vanity turned. I felt myself tumbling.

My body rocketed toward the ground. The wind rushed in my face as I was catapulted from my body over buildings and across town. Gradually, my flight arced. Below me, I saw the man and several others. The roof and floor of the barbershop bowed and unhinged in scattered, pixelated platelets.

The concrete floor raced closer and closer. I tensed, bracing for impact. But suddenly, my body stopped. My hair skimmed the ground inches from my face. I pushed onto the space above the ground and stood as if walking on air.

"Quickly, Kiera. What do you see?" Minerva asked.

The man stood with his back to me. Crimson robes hid his face, but I could tell by his monstrous frame and height that it was him. Candles lit the basement's interior. A giant iron symbol of a whiskered serpent, cradling a globe in a nest, hung on the wall.

The men gathered and stood before a podium. The barbershop clerk stood center stage with his hood back. Something was different about him. His eyes glowed pupil less and white. He spoke in two languages at once.

"Brothers, the mother marilyth has gathered her clutch to discuss recent attacks."

The men hissed like snakes.

"As you all know, she relies on you to weed out the sinister conspirator against us."

I moved past the men in the crowd. It was as if I was invisible, traceless and elusive. I could move through bodies but remained tethered to him by an unseen force.

"Present the conspirator."

A hooded figure uncurled a wanted poster of a fanged creature with horns and scales like mine.

My thug spoke up. "I have seen this one, my lady. She was snooping around the back this morning."

"Step forward."

I felt tugged along like a balloon behind him onto the stage.

He knelt before the clerk.

As I neared the clerk, I noticed that his eyes never blinked. In fact, behind them, a ghostly clerk clamored from inside them to be freed, as if possessed.

"And what did you do with her?" both voices asked.

"I . . . I let her go."

"You what?"

The thug's hood was pulled back. A spectral snake loomed behind the clerk, ready to devour him. The serpent's head skirted the ceiling. Two stems jutted from its back and long barbed whiskers. It looked like the symbol behind it. The thug couldn't see it, though, the vision only appeared to me.

"Forgive me, my queen, I—"

"Inconceivable!" The snake's mouth moved as did the clerk's. "You know your penalty."

The thug pleaded for his life. The clerk pulled out an obsidian dagger. The cult began incessantly chanting, "Death!" over and over.

"Hurry up, Kiera. I don't know how much longer I can hold this," Minnie said.

The snake tilted its neck toward the shattered ceiling and looked me in the eye. I saw her furrowed brow soften. She opened her mouth in shock and smiled, with three rows of teeth starting from the back of her throat.

The clerk began to speak with his own voice.

"What's that? Yes, yes, perhaps there *is* some use for him."

The serpent lunged. Its tentacles curled and entangled my spirit. Its gaping mouth vacuumed me into a vortex of venomous teeth. My body was stunned.

"Behold!" The beast spoke in doubles. "The accused!"

A crystal ball was brought front and center. It glowed and flashed three figures beneath the library around the looking glass: Minnie, me, and a spectral wolf of cloud hovering over my shoulder.

"The library! Go! Now! Do not fail us."

Immediately, the men scattered. My spirit fell limp beneath the snake.

The clerk and his queen stood over me. "Foolish girl. You know nothing about the powers you play with. We shall bring about your demise."

Minnie began shouting. "Kiera, you're bleeding. Kiera? That's it! We're done here."

My body shook as Minnie yanked me by the shoulders away from the mirror. Blood trickled from my nose. My wrists seemed slit as well. Whatever had happened to my spiritual form had also hurt my physical form.

Minnie wiped the blood away from my nose with a hankie and hugged me tight.

"I'm sorry. I'm sorry. I'm sorry," she whispered over and over.

"I'm fine. It's not your fault."

"I didn't know you were allergic to the mysts. And—"

Her eyes caught my wrists. She pushed me into the chair and sent it across the room, leaving skid marks before my head hit the wall.

"What did you see?" she demanded.

"I . . . I don't know."

I felt a knot rising on the back of my head.

"Liar!" Her voice boomed like thunder.

"Really. I don't know. There was a cult, a snake, and a wolf—here in the library. All I know is we need to leave now. They're coming for me, and they're coming for you, possibly, too."

"No, I'm not going anywhere. These cuts are marks of dark magic. I thought we were friends!"

With her shout, a series of books flew across the room. A whistling windstorm surrounded Minerva. Her hair rose as if pulled into a cyclone. Her eyes bulged in anger. A sword flew off the mantle and she caught it in her hand.

"Who are you? Talk!"

"Okay. Okay. My name's not Kiera. It's Sinopa. I've run away from home. My first night here I was framed for murder and now everyone wants me dead. First the cops, now these cult guys. Please don't hurt me. I'm sorry. I've got no family and nowhere to turn."

I curled into a ball. The winds died down. I peeked at her and saw that her hair laid down but with static. She strapped the sword to her thigh under her skirt and stretched her hand out to me.

I cautiously took it. She clenched my hand and pulled me into an embrace so hard it cracked my back. My heart pounded. I felt pretty sure I was dead.

She let go, and her voice mellowed to its normal, perky tone.

"You're wrong. Take your charcoal, we're leaving."

"You believe me?"

"I'm an avid reader, aren't I? Your walls are down. I told you to be real with me. But if you lie to me again, they won't find a body."

I nodded.

"Tell me what you saw. Where were they?"

"The barbershop in Southtown."

"They'll be here any minute, then. Can you walk?"

I rose to my feet. My stomach felt better, but my legs felt off balance. I stumbled as if walking for the first time.

Minnie *tsk-tsked*.

"Eat your charcoal. I'll pack my purse. We're in for quite a fight."

"Fight? Shouldn't we run away? There had to be fifty of them, and there's two of us."

Minnie ignored me. She sang to herself and combed through her wardrobe, stuffing a small shoulder bag. "You know, Kiki . . ."

I still wasn't fond of that name.

"This looks like so much fun. It's been a century since I went adventuring."

I swallowed another tablet, staring down at the cuts on my wrists. They stung when I touched them. It was the exact same symbol that had been hanging on the wall.

"Don't pick at them, dearie. You've been marked."

She grabbed another bottle of alcohol and poured it over my cuts. It stung, with steam rising from my wounds. I cried out in pain.

The marks melted, and immediately the wounds sealed as if they had never been there at all. I rubbed my wrists.

"Ouch. That hurt."

"Hurts me, too. That was perfectly good brandy. She can't track you now."

"The serpent—who is she?"

Minnie shook her head.

"The great Wyrm Queen is a dark plague to this city, a marilyth. They prey on magicians and leech off their life in exchange for power. That's why I wear this ring."

A white moonstone band was wrapped around her pinky.

"Moonstone acts like water. I'm invisible."

"You wouldn't happen to have a second one, would you?"

She rubbed her chin for a moment and raced for her jewelry box. The drawers slammed open and shut. She kicked the dresser in frustration.

"Afraid not." She sighed, opened the bottom drawer, and stuffed her purse. "Ready to go?"

"Hardly. You don't seem to understand me here. They have an army."

"And I have a book cart and the Dewey Decimal system. What's your point?"

"That's not very reassuring."

"Lacking confidence, I see. Take this."

Her fingers scavenged through her purse and she tossed me a small gold canister.

"Lipstick?"

"It's got salt lick in it, too. Knock 'em dead, kiddo."

I laughed. She took my arm over her shoulder.

"Lighten up, dearie. Smile."

"At least I won't die ugly."

"That's the spirit."

CHAPTER FOURTEEN

The basement door creaked open. Minnie's head swiveled around the corner.

"We'll get Nigel to summon the guard. Hide under my desk. In the chaos, we'll slip you out the front door. Should things go awry, we'll meet in the office and come up with a new plan."

"You really think this is going to work?"

"We'll see. Remember, if they get a hold of you, knock 'em dead."

By now, we had reached her desk.

"But, wait, I don't see what lipstick is gonna—"

"Quick! Get down!"

"What?"

"Shh, someone's coming."

I propped my back against the underside of the desk. At least, with my height, I didn't have to crunch my neck too much. Darkness clouded my vision. I could see the hem of Minnie's dress on one side and light seeping underneath the slit at the bottom.

I lay flat to peek under where the desk met the floor for a better look. A pair of muddy boots heavily pounded toward the desk. Then another. And another, until there were three pairs, each releasing clods of dirt on the checkered tiles.

Minnie's heels approached the side of the desk. One foot nervously itched the back of the other. She cleared her throat.

"Hello, gentlemen, what may I do for you today?"

A spit wad smacked against the floor as one hocked a loogie. A woman spoke.

"We're looking for someone—a girl about four-foot-eight, red scales, and wide around the hips. Seen anybody like that?"

I bit my tongue. First of all, I was at least four-foot-ten, thank you very much.

"Nope. Haven't seen her. Sorry."

There was a moment of silence. The boots to the left and right began circling out of sight.

"Skank is lying. You can see it in her eyes. Textbook. I suggest you cooperate."

"I don't know what you're talking about. But please watch your language, this is a family establishment."

Minnie shrieked. Her legs flailed in the air.

"And what if I don't?" challenged the woman's voice.

Minnie choked. "Then I'm going to have to ask you to leave."

The woman laughed. Minnie crashed into her swivel chair and flipped over on her back. Her glasses hit the floor.

"Those who harbor criminals are just as guilty as the criminals themselves. I hope you have a good lawyer."

"My glasses. I can't see."

"Take her with us. She might prove useful for finding this basement your employer spoke of."

A man came behind and pulled Minnie over to the other side of the desk.

"Let go of me. Help! Nigel! Help! Someone? Anyone."

"Put a sock in it."

Minnie squealed then. Then her cries muffled.

"Play nice, and we let you go, nice and easy-like. Nigel's been relieved of duty, by the way."

Why doesn't she use magic? She could take them.

My guess was the men pulled her away. I was alone.

92

The woman sighed.

Or so I thought.

Her boots paced over to my left. I could see her out of the corner of my eye. Her hair draped long and brown past her shoulders. She pulled it behind her ears, away from her eyes. Her lips were dyed a dark purple.

I stayed perfectly still.

Her strides were wide. Her steps were heavy and weighted in her pace. They echoed like a ticking clock.

Clip. Clop. Clip. Clop. Like a leaky faucet.

She moved closer.

Clip. Clop. Clip. Clop.

She entered behind the horseshoe desk.

I held my breath.

One of the thugs snickered some distance off. Minnie whined. She was still close, thank heavens. The woman's back was turned to me. I sat up and pressed my back against the side of one of the walls.

The woman snapped, "Hey, try something funny like that again and they'll have to sew your lips back on. Understand? I don't care how much you're paying me. She may not be human, but they have feelings."

She shook her head, bent over, picked up Minnie's glasses, and blew them off. "I don't get paid enough for this," she muttered to herself.

I could see from this angle that one of her ears came up to a point. My back slid against the wall for a better look. My tail thumped against the top of the desk.

"Ouch," I blurted out. *Oops.*

Her head turned and our eyes locked.

"Too easy," she said as she smiled at me.

I rolled out from under the desk.

"This way!" she called out.

The two men each held one of Minnie's arms behind her back. Immediately, in a burst of wind, they plowed into the side of the bookshelves and she struggled with her gag.

"Kiera, run!"

I vaulted the desk and did my best to run. My body felt it had only just stabilized.

"Useless," the woman groaned. "I'll do this myself."

Over my shoulder, I heard footfalls gaining fast.

I turned the corner of a bookshelf. Two more cultists. I darted down another aisle.

"After her! Alive, now, remember?"

A book cart rested at the other side of the hall. I leaned on the shelves for balance. The men laughed at how "the wyrm would eat well."

My heart sank. I could almost hear them breathing down my neck. I turned and shoved the cart as hard as I could. Two of the men tumbled backward on the ground. The woman leapfrogged it and rolled forward, undeterred.

I turned down another aisle and tossed books behind me off the shelves, hoping one would hit her. I was too scared to turn around and aim. My back pressed against the end of a shelf. My lungs heaved. Dizziness set in. The drugs still hadn't entirely worn off.

Nothing but silence. My head peeked around the way I came. A trail of books was strewn about the floor, but there was no one in pursuit.

Where'd the lady go?

"Oh, changeling?" she called out mockingly.

My fingers snatched the nearest book off the shelf I could reach. Luckily, it was a heavy dictionary. Thank God for Webster.

"Oh, Miss Changeling, do please come out. Give yourself up, and I promise I won't hurt you or your friend."

I struggled to catch my breath. The room turned and blurred as if in a funhouse mirror. A ghostly figure stood at the end of the shelf with a finger to his lips. He was tall, lanky, and human. Thick-rimmed glasses sat on his face and a pasty white coat wrapped around his torso.

He gestured for me to follow.

I heard footsteps approaching. *Clip. Clop. Clip. Clop.* As she turned the corner, I swung my book, bashing her in the nose. As she grabbed her face, I swung again, and she fell to the ground. my arms wildly tossed the book, and I ran in a blind panic.

The figure waved for me to follow. I fled the other direction.

Who can I trust?

Everything moved so fast. Bookshelves fell on top of each other like dominos. Blurs shouted and raced all around me.

As I reached the end of an aisle, the white-coated figure appeared before me like a ghost, with his hand out for me to stop. I slowed so as not to run into him, and five cultists raced past the other end with a book-keeper in hot pursuit. Had I run any further, I'd have been a goner.

Before I could thank him, I was sent reeling to the ground. The world turned. A cultist juggled three books suspended in the air above him. One by one they swooshed, hammering me to the floor. I crawled away on my back. More flew off the shelves and bruised my skin. Then his muddy boot stomped my throat. I pulled at his ankle for air.

"You've slain our brethren in cold blood. The wyrm queen will have her revenge. You will pay with your life now or later."

I gagged and wheezed for air. The blood drained from my face. His body towered over me. Part of his underwear stuck out the leg of his shorts. My tail swung and punched him in the groin. I needed air. I floundered away on my knees like a landed fish.

He struck me from behind again. His knees pinned my shoulders to the floor.

"You're going to pay for that."

My nose bashed into the floor and my eyes watered. I struggled to keep them open. My tail couldn't make contact with him again. Blood poured from my busted lip. I heard Minnie shout behind me and wind rushed past.

DONG.

A book cart flew end over end and the man fell limp at my side. A giant knot set upon his noggin. Minnie pulled me to my feet to keep going. My vision blurred. The next thing I knew, we were underground. She was holding a wet rag to my head and telling me everything would be all right.

CHAPTER FIFTEEN

Thumping and shouting echoed above us. An iron gate creaked. Minnie lit a torch.

"Kiera, stay with me now."

"Where are we?"

"Weren't you paying attention earlier? I have maps of the old sewer system, remember?"

"That explains the smell."

Minnie hunched down to my level, inspecting me with her torch. The middle of her snout had dried blood, and the end of her skirt was soaked in sewage. "How do you feel?"

"Less dizzy. My nose hurts now, though."

"It's a wonder it's not broken."

"That man who helped me—who was he?"

"What man?"

"The one in the lab coat and glasses."

"I didn't see any man, Kiera."

"There was a man. He was right there. He stopped me from running into a whole bunch of thugs."

"Hmm, I don't know. Maybe you have a guardian angel."

"Oh, very funny."

"Kiera, if you don't mind, I think it's best we keep moving. If they could see you before, who's to say they can't now? It's said that mari-lyths are powerful enough to ignore the whole water interference thing."

"Really?"

She nodded. "Although it's not been proven, I don't want to be the one to find out, if you know what I mean."

Minnie helped me to my feet. My balance had been restored. My vision cleared.

"You passed out briefly. I had to carry you down here."

"How long was I out?

"About an hour, maybe more. You slept like a baby. It felt terrible to wake you."

We walked along a concrete path beside a green waterway. The tunnel's ceiling arched above us, and droplets fell from it. The sound of trickling water and creaking bounced off the walls.

Minnie led the way with determination. For once, she was silent. The feeling set in that perhaps I had misjudged her.

"Thank you," I said.

"For what?"

"You didn't have to do that."

"Don't mention it. Anything for a fellow reader, and more impor-tantly, a friend."

"Thank you."

"I do expect you to keep these tunnels secret if you don't mind."

"Why?"

She turned around and smiled. "You'll see. Promise?"

I nodded.

She clapped her hands together.

"Oh, goody!"

The tunnel eventually arrived at a levy blocking the water flow.

We dropped down and followed it on the wider path. Soon, we arrived at a wide room with metal grates comprising the floor. A few dim bulbs flickered overhead. A large basin took up the center of the room with a small one within it. Twelve gates and tunnels branched out of the room, aligned with hydrant shaped pedestals. A dull-colored crystal orb rested on the top of each hydrant.

"Welcome to the Kakata waterway. These devices control the levies and the flow of freshwater and sanitation of wastewater throughout the city. Supposedly, they even line up the army's mines. It was an ambitious project. Sadly, the city abandoned most of the system when the keys mysteriously disappeared."

She pulled a ring of rusted keys from her purse and placed them in my hand.

"Care to do the honors?"

"What do you want me to do?"

"Unlock levy six. I'll run upstairs behind us, pull the lever, and we'll follow the tunnel to the east district. A friend of mine can help us there." Minnie tugged at the tarnished copper gate behind us.

I inserted the key into the rusted mechanism and yanked at the hydrant with all my might. A faint click sounded behind me.

"Minnie? Is everything all right?"

Her heels slipped and she slid down the damp steps.

"You okay?"

She dusted herself off. "Never better. What seems to be the problem, love?"

"The thing's stuck""

Minnie spat on her hands, moved in front of me and said, "Step aside."

With a grunt, the orb glowed white. The main turned with a squeal. The basin filled. A door to tunnel six rose slowly, with chains.

"Just needed a little elbow grease," Minnie chuckled.

Her arms were practically toothpicks compared to mine. Something was screwy. I knew I could trust her, but then again, she did drug me. Who was she really?

She stepped down ahead toward the gate. "Ready to go?"

"Wait. Before, at the library, those guys said you're a sorceress?"

She smirked. "You could say I dabble a bit, yes."

"Why didn't you fight back?"

"Quite frankly, dear, I'm exhausted. Let's walk and talk. Scrying twice in one day, I feel I'll shrivel up and die. I've already done too much. Had anyone seen what I did, I'd lose my job. I'd be a hex offender and be branded as such for life. At worst, I'd be executed. Iron bracelets aren't my style."

"But it was in self-defense."

"Says who? Me? Don't be so naïve, dear. Remember, people don't take to our kind very well. I don't even have a permit to practice. No, I did what I had to."

I still wasn't buying it but kept quiet.

Slime and sludge oozed from the walls. The fumes stung my nostrils. Large piping hung above us. The occasional rat scurried overhead.

"It won't be much longer. It's just around this."

A light flickered in the distance. Shadows cast on the paths above us. Maroon robes crept closer in the darkness.

"Change of plans. This way."

We began running the way we came.

"How did they find us?"

"Quiet! They'll hear you. We gotta hide."

Two faint lights approached on both sides of the tunnel above us. The remaining water splashed at our ankles. To our left was a sealed hatch. Minnie groaned, pulling the wheel.

The light raced toward us. I yanked as hard as I could. The iron hatch creaked. My feet slipped and I plunged into the water behind me. I choked. It quickly drained and the hatch gargled.

Shouts rose from the cultists.

"On your feet, Kiera." Minnie chucked her torch as far as she could and it sizzled in the still water. Darkness set in immediately. She pulled me toward the hatch. Water trickled beneath us. My old fears sank in. Rushing back, they hit me all at once.

"What are you waiting for? We don't have time for this."

She pushed me in. I screamed. My body barreled down the pipe. The grease-covered walls propelled me like a rocket. I plunged into the murky depths.

Sound muffled. My limbs flailed. I needed air. I was trapped. Another object crashed in the sea of black. Something grabbed my waist. I flailed harder, smacking and pushing away. It pulled me to the surface, and I coughed, breathing in deep.

"What's gotten into you?" Minnie scolded. "That hurt."

"Get me out. I can't swim."

"Not with that form, no. Calm down. You're only pushing yourself down."

"I can't swim. I can't see."

"Don't tell me you're afraid of water."

My elbow struck her ribs. I drifted away. My head bobbed barely above the surface.

"Get me out now!"

"You are! You are afraid of water, aren't you?" she giggled.

My lips took on water and I gargled.

"All right, all right." Minnie pulled me to the surface again and snapped at me not to hit her.

She helped me swim to the side and I could feel the cold metal bars of a ladder. I climbed up with all my strength and choked on the water in my lungs. My clothes stuck to my back. I nearly froze in the frigid underground.

Minnie chuckled to herself. "My, you're like a frightened little rabbit."

"Am not!" I coughed. I did my best to raise my voice.

"Right." She snickered.

"You think this is funny? You could have killed me."

"Sweet pea, I've lost no one under my wing. Rest assured, you couldn't be safer in a bank vault than with me. Come now. Let's get going. It's only a matter of time before they find you again. Come along. On your feet, dearest."

Her wet feet smacked on the stone. I assumed she had lost her heels in the fall.

"You want to continue? How can you see? We lost the torch, remember?"

Her footsteps came back to me. "You're telling me you can't?"

She was six inches from my face and I couldn't even tell. Her hands lifted my face to look her in the eye.

"Hormones have done you wrong, child. Don't worry. I can tell you'll get it eventually. You've got the spark and the goods. You're just missing a catalyst. My, you're a special read, darling. I can't make heads or tails of you. Come now, if you stay here too long, you'll catch a cold."

She helped me to my feet and held my hand in the dark. I only took it because I was blind otherwise. The water sloshed beneath us as it rose and fell. We were enveloped in darkness. I couldn't see my hand in front of my face, and it didn't matter how far away it was.

"So, Kiera?"

"What is it this time?"

"Why are you afraid of water?"

"I'm not."

"Oh, come on. Humor an old lady, will you? We've got time to kill. Childhood trauma, perhaps?"

"No."

Minnie laughed.

"Why so sour, spoil sport? Your eyes darted to the left, by the way. Want to try that again?"

I shook my head.

Why did Max have to ditch me with her?

"Now do me. Ask me something."

"All right. Where are we heading? We've been meandering in these tunnels forever."

Minnie sighed. "Gotta take the wind out of my sails, don't you? It was meant as a surprise, but I trust you. My hoard leads to the surface under the library."

"Your what?"

"No, no, no. Wait and see. I feel you are gonna love it."

We came to a door with a dim light flickering at the end of the hall and overhead. Tarnished copper inlays sat out from the door. "Keep out" was written in fifteen different languages. Carvings of a creature mirrored both sides, playing sentinel. It flew with four wings: one pair avian and the other reptilian. A plumed tail draped the ground, and from its lizard head it breathed pure voltage.

Minnie placed her hand on the door and the metal glowed. Two metal bars ground and slid. The door creaked open, no longer barring our passage. Minnie gestured for me to go first.

"Please, after you. I don't get many visitors. Make yourself at home."

I eyed her uneasily. My boot sloshed sewer water past the door frame.

The room felt even colder than the tunnel. Not a single light. The door shut behind us.

"Oh, where are my manners?" Minnie clapped her hands together. Candles flickered in tints of blue. A haze clouded the floor. Strange, glowing white stone coated the walls. Massive heaps of gold coins and trinkets rose like mountains in the corners of the enormous room. Each pile was sorted neatly and arranged alphabetically by the Dewey Decimal System.

How on Earth she managed to keep it straight that way was beyond me, but it was best not to ask questions. Because questions led to Motor-mouth Minnie flapping away about the "exquisite intricacies" of her precious sorting system for nine hours.

"Pardon the mess. Please, make yourself at home and try not to touch anything," she said.

CHAPTER SIXTEEN

"This is all yours?"

"Minus what's in the bank, but yes. I'm a bit of a collector. Hoarder, really. I have no friends, dearie. What else am I supposed to do with my time? Crochet?"

I stared in awe. Stalactites hung, carved with murals of winged tendril serpents, giant plated pangolins, four-winged dragons, and fiery phoenixes. Crystal chandeliers hung over piles of rubies. Exotic rugs covered my every step.

"Well, don't just stand there. Come in, come in. Moonstone lines the walls; she can't see us here. Care for a tour?"

"Would I?!"

She took me by the arm and led me inside. From that moment, her lips never stopped flapping. Every item had a story that she simply couldn't bear for me not to hear.

"You want to see my most prized treasures before you go. I have a small chimney there to dry off."

I nodded.

Every sight was a wonder: ruby-eyed statues, blankets of phoenix feathers, opals like saucers. What could possibly be her most prized jewels?

I was taken into a study nearly identical to the one in her office. She got a small fire going, reassuring me she piped the smoke to her office. Apparently, we were directly below it.

"This is the restricted section. These are the books closed off to the public for being too dangerous in knowledge and politics."

Shelves lined the walls. Multi-colored spines faced us. I couldn't help but feel disappointed.

"That's it? You have a literal ton of gold outside and these are your most prized possessions."

Minnie sighed. "I don't expect you to understand. It's not the paper that makes them valuable but the ideas behind them. The feelings that they invoke. Surely, you must have a story that means something to you?"

She gestured for us to sit in the wicker chair by the fire. I shivered on my knees instead.

"Well, don't you? You seemed enamored with the books upstairs."

"I do. *The Ugly Duckling*. My brother read it to me when I was little."

"See, I told—"

"I dreamed that one day I'd find my true family. Someplace I'd belong. Till then, I'd just have to wait and see."

Minnie cleared her throat. "I'm sorry."

"It's okay. It's not your fault."

"Now you see the power reading can have for humanity. It is a shame even a single book should be lost. Pick any book. Any one and it's yours."

"Oh, Minnie, I couldn't."

"Nonsense. We're friends now, right?"

"Yes, but—"

"I'll choose for you. Here. You wanted to know more about mari-lyths, didn't you?"

She handed me a small, worn, vellum book bound in leather.

"*The Pocket Edition Guide to the Arcane and Post-Post-Apocalyptic Beasts, volume three*. My favorite."

"Minnie, I can't take this."

"Nonsense. I've practically memorized it. I've scribed it into a note-book myself. The information must be put to proper use. You could certainly use it— a young sorceress like yourself being chased by a big ugly snake. Best not to look a gift horse in the mouth."

"But I—"

"No buts. I won't hear another word about it. Of course, you'll be needing this if you are checking it out."

She handed me a brass stamped library card.

"Lifetime membership is rather pricey, but I'll waive it for a friend. I'm the head librarian. What are they going to do? Fire me? Ha. I'd like to see the bigwigs try."

As usual, I couldn't get a word in.

She sat beside me by the fire and wrung her hair out.

I threw my arms around her. "Thank you."

Her ears tucked back in surprise but returned the embrace. "Don't mention it, dearie."

After we had dried off, more crashes echoed above us. Minnie chewed her bottom lip. "That wyrm better back down if she knows what's good for her. Let's get you out of here."

She handed me a dry map. In the corner, two iron ladders rose from the wall. We took the ladder and Minnie pushed up a manhole cover. Her head swiveled like a periscope. "Coast's clear. Hurry."

I brushed the dirt off my dress. As Minnie pushed the heavy lid over the hole, three men approached in the alley. A brick wall boxed us in from behind.

"Well, well, well. Nowhere to run. Poor, poor girls. Shouldn't have worked up the wyrm's appetite. I hear she likes to play with her food before eating."

Their shadows cast over us. I slowly backed up to the wall. Minnie dropped the manhole cover and looked up. Flames flickered from a man's fingertips.

"Now, we can do this the easy way or the hard way."

Minnie backed up with her arms out, shielding me.

"Step aside, lady, or you're next."

"If she goes, I go."

One man snickered. He pulled the dagger from his cloak. "My pleasure."

The head cultist spoke again. "Surrender now. Don't make this any harder than it is."

"You swear not to hurt her?"

The man nodded.

"Minnie, what are you doing?" I gasped.

"Turning myself in," she said with a wink.

She extended her wrists to them.

They extinguished their magic and lowered their weapons. Manacles were slapped onto Minnie's wrists. She pulled them both by the throat and blew a sugary white cloud. The guards fell to the ground, out cold. The head cultist loaded a tiny crossbow.

Minnie charged with a scream. He dropped his bow. Her foot bashed his groin in. He fell to his knees, cupping his crotch. She grabbed both his cheeks and kissed him goodnight. Another white cotton cloud whisked him off to sleep. Minnie grabbed her head in pain. I rushed to her side.

She chuckled to herself. "It seems old age is creeping up on me. I could use a nap myself."

"That was amazing."

"You best get moving, love. They'll be looking for you. Go to Sophia's store, on the east side."

"You all right?"

"A little tired, that's all. I've been scrying . . . and this." She stood up and cracked her back.

"What about them?"

She lifted two by the collars. "We'll just have a little chat, that's all. I'd like to see what they know. A little hot tea and cookies will loosen the tongue. Maybe we can get to know each other better. After all, I'm an excellent hostess."

"That you are."

I stared at her frail form, easily lifting twice her weight.

"Who are you really?'

Minnie smirked. "Oh, just a librarian. Just like you're only a girl named Kiera."

I hugged her again and raced off into the street. I made my way to the theater district, as it was the quickest path to the docks. The mummers juggled on the street corner like before, and flutists piped on the other. With any luck, I could make it across town without being stopped by anyone.

"Hey, miss, remember me?" said a small voice with a tugging at my cloak.

Too late. I looked down. There was Simon. He was in full, oversized pants and suspenders like before, and a tiny black leather top hat.

I nodded and smiled, trying my best to remain polite. I checked over my shoulders for cultists. Simon put on another magic show for me, failing again to draw the right card. He made a small ball bearing levitate and bounce between his palms. The thought of the cultists being anywhere near us set me on edge. I had to leave. I had to get to Minnie's friend.

"Hey, are you watching?"

"Sorry. It's very neat, Simon."

"Oh, that's just kid stuff. I'm sure you can do better."

"Well, I don't know how."

"Don't know how? Come on. I'll show ya."

"Simon, I don't think that's such a—"

He looked up at me with puppy dog eyes. I couldn't say no.

"All right, fine. But only for a little while. I need to get to a store called Sophia's."

"Hey, that's my house. Oh, goody! You can stay for lunch. Mother will be so glad to have company."

Simon skipped—well, tried to skip—in his oversized pants, leading the way. The whole time, I couldn't help but think about what Romero had said. I remembered how magic was dangerous, how people couldn't be trusted, and people weren't meant to wield such power. Then I remembered how played I felt. What did he know? I set out to prove him wrong.

Still, I couldn't shake the worry his tale had created in me. Simon ran back and led me by the hand. Fancy that—I was so hopeless that a child had to lead me along. It's a good thing Angela wasn't there to see that.

Simon brought me to a two-story building with a thatched roof. It was built of stone, like the others, but the stones were varied, as it had been rebuilt time and time again. Above the door was a sign, "Sophia's Sundries and Sorcery." A small bell rang as the door opened.

"Mom, I'm home," Simon called out.

The room looked like a typical drug store, with dry and canned goods for sale on the shelves and hats on the rack. The only unusual thing to note was a black curtain covering the entrance to the back room.

A short lady appeared from behind the curtain. She shared the same small button-nose and tousled hair as Simon. Her bony fingers tightened her apron before rushing to her register.

"What can I do you for?" she asked. Her smile curled, forming her cheeks into soft pear halves.

"Oh, no, I don't need anything," I said.

"Mom, you know why she's here, silly."

Simon's mom batted her hand, smiling.

"Wait, so you know why I'm here?"

"No. But I saw you with Simon across town. So, what are you here for?"

I shuddered at the thought of being watched, and so far away, too.

"I'm looking for Sophia, and, well, Simon said you would show me how to do the magical thing-ily—uh—thing."

As you are very aware, I have a way with words.

The lady smiled.

"Mother's busy at the moment, but I'll be more than happy to help you in the meantime."

"I'm kind of in a hurry and don't have the coin to buy anything right now."

I regretted not asking Minnie for some of her hoard.

"Nonsense. Poverty is no excuse not to be a patron of the arts." She placed her arm around my shoulder and began leading me into the back room.

"It's not that. It's just—I—"

Inside, dim candlelight glowed in the room. Glass vials full of fluids of many colors lined the shelves. Rows of banana tree leaves hung on the walls. A large glass chandelier hung suspended above a raised platform, which stood in the middle of the room with an iron-barred grate in the center.

"Sorry for the mess," she said, "Festivals are *busy*."

She reached out for the mop and bucket across the room. Condensation formed around her wrist. She clenched her fist and the mop stood up and shot toward her. My jaw dropped.

"That was incredible!"

"Thank you, dearie. That was nothing, really. I'm sure someone born with the spark or shimmer like yourself can do plenty more."

"What's the shimmer?"

"You really don't know?"

I shook my head. I was growing tired of that question today.

"Well, back in the olden days when the mysts were ripe, people began to learn the powers of the mysts. They experienced the magnificent beasts birthed from its haze, and the gifts it would bring to some. Those born with the innate ability to control the mysts were noted as having a glimmer or 'the spark' in their pupils. Usually at birth, but sometimes not until adolescence. And those sapphire cat eyes of yours, my dear, are simply glowing."

I blushed.

"You have a gift, dear. Now, let's see. We'll start small. Simon, hand me one of my ball bearings, will you? I know you took them. I saw you do it."

The boy sighed, took off his top hat, and dug through his pockets. He slowly raised a small pouch out and trudged over to place it in her hand. She handed me a ball bearing.

"A little faster next time, please. Thank you. Right. Anyway, I want you to focus on the ball. Take slow, deep breaths and visualize what you want the ball to do. You want it to float between your hands. You got that?"

I nodded. I heard the bell jingle outside. Simon's mother said she'd be right back, and if I had questions, to ask him.

I stood transfixed on the tiny ball. I lifted my hand and moved it occasionally, hoping a different angle might help. Simon stood waiting anxiously. A minute passed. Then two minutes. I squinted. I asked Simon for another ball from the sack, but still nothing. Simon slumped to the floor. I could tell he was getting bored.

Simon's mother came back in through the curtain, leading Hazel along behind her.

"Ha. It seems Old Slim is still into witchy women, then."

"Romero?" I asked.

Hazel laughed. "Romero? Is that what he's going by now? Yeah, Old Slim always chased up broomsticks, so to speak."

I wasn't sure how to feel. All his warnings about the danger, did he even follow them?

"Any luck, dearie?" Simon's mother asked.

I shook my head.

She walked over to the giant platform in the middle of the room. "Hazel, darling, would you mind locking the front door?" Hazel left out the curtain. "Well, miss, sorry—I realized I never got your name."

"Kiera."

"Kiera, that's a pretty name. Mine's Cheryl. Yes, Miss Kiera, I believe it may be from one of two things. One, you are not of the age. Or two, and this is one more likely, there's simply not enough myst for you to draw from."

Cheryl moved over to a giant lever on the other side of the platform with a tiny furnace.

"So, with your permission, I'd like to test the second."

I stared down the ominously oversized lever. Smoke lightly smoldered out the furnace pipes. I rubbed my wrists. "Is it safe?"

Cheryl laughed. "You're a big girl. I think you can handle it. I'll be with you every step of the way if you can't. It's only dangerous if you don't know what you're doing. We're above ground. I think we know what we're doing, and—Simon!"

All eyes turned to him, shuddering with a bar of chocolate in his hands.

"Those are for the guests. You'll spoil your supper."

"But Mom, I was just—"

"No buts. Besides, you know you're not supposed to be here when Mommy's working. Hazel, dear, do you mind? Just make sure he stays out of trouble. You can stay in here when you're old enough to handle it."

Simon sighed and slumped. He shuffled across the tile floor. Hazel escorted the small trudging boy out the curtain, leaving me alone without a familiar face to lean on.

Cheryl asked, "Ready?"

I shook my head. She laughed and threw the switch anyway. Her hand beckoned me over to the platform. As I approached, I could see the inside was hollow. Metal blades opened, revealing a shaft with a whirling blade.

Myst began rising. Steam filled the room. A sticky humidity poured in. Moisture flickered the candles.

My lungs starved for oxygen. I couldn't breathe. My palms began to sweat. I felt tension in my muscles. My knees gave out.

"You!" a voice shouted from the darker smoke billowing from the hole. "You've returned."

My skin leaped. I crawled away from the shaft. I felt inexplicably hot. The figure of a wolf head rose from the shaft. I hyperventilated. My chest tightened with every breath. My heart raced. Sweat dripped from my brow. A silhouette crept closer in the fog.

"I am coming for you. Yes, my daughter, I'm coming soon."

My throat began to burn hotter and hotter. It began to glow. I snuffed the light with my hands.

A shadow grabbed my shoulder in the myst. I screamed. Cheryl shook me. Her lips moved, but no words came. I heard a sizzling. I shook my hands. They were scalded with blisters. I felt heat boil from my pits and loins.

The room spun. Cheryl tilted in double above me. A roaring growl shook the room. My eyes shot to the shaft. A frothy smoke squall massed as a looming dark canine head.

It spoke, "I'm coming!"

The head rose and snaked forward in a beeline. It chanted as it bulleted toward me, "They'll pay." Over and over, coming closer, "They'll pay."

The clouds swallowed me whole and I screamed. I felt my head hit the concrete and limply roll to one side. A figure loomed in shadow. My breath still fluttered as I lay on my back.

My eyelids lowered, blinking open only slightly. I fought to stay awake. The figure brushed my hair away and slapped my cheeks. I gave in. Darkness was all I saw. My eyelids came down. I lay to rest.

CHAPTER SEVENTEEN

The next thing I knew, I stood in a dark room. The voice continued to speak, only softer now, and gentle. The gruffness and temper had left.

"Welcome home, my daughter."

His voice cooed, soft and gentle, and spoke ubiquitously without a source. I felt pulled forward. A dim light shone on a walkway.

"How I've longed for the one who got away. The bones of my bones," it spoke over my shoulder.

"Who are you?" I called out.

I turned to see nothing. Nothing but darkness. I was alone in an empty void.

Whatever it was, the shadows hid it well. The ground shook in front of me. Lights blinked one by one. Before me, eight carved stone statues glowed from underneath. As I approached, an ominous song began. First low, with one voice, and then slowly escalating as more voices joined one by one in a chorus.

"Yes, that's it, my daughter. Approach your destiny. Only you can open it."

I tried to ask what he meant, but my lips only quivered. It froze me where I stood. I tried to turn back. My boots stuck to the floor. I desperately struggled to move my arms, but a force held me in place as if a weight held me down from my shoulders. The statues' eyes smoldered red. The voices got louder and louder.

"Fulfill your role, your birthright! Open the door!" the voice shouted.

I begged to understand, but my throat squeezed silent. Not a peep, not a sound came from my lips. The jaws of the statues opened, and the song blared in stereo all around me.

"Open the door. Fulfill your duty. This is our calling, our victory. It is yours; take it. We will serve justice. Do it. Do it now."

The song grew louder, drowning out all my thoughts. Darkness poured from the mouths of the statues like water. I could feel it grip my ankles and climb my legs. I was drowning. My body desperately shrugged and shook, trying to be free of this weight. It strangled my waist, wrenching it tight. Tears poured from my eyes.

"Open the door quickly. Come to me. You'll be safe,"

My head shot upward, pulled like a fish dangling from a hook. I couldn't look down. The muck rose and crawled up my skin. I felt it creep and rise to my collar.

The ichor whipped from my neck, splashing to my lips. I couldn't move. I couldn't breathe. My lungs gasped for air. The sludge yanked my chin down. Finally, it reached my face. It trickled up my cheeks. I screamed, but not a sound escaped my lips. The darkness consumed me whole.

I shot up, awake. The sun shined on my face. I rubbed my eyes. My sides shook and I discovered that I was bundled up in a quilt. My head swelled as if it would split wide open.

Sweat rolled from my forehead, and I'd soiled my pants. I felt disgusting. I groaned as I tried to sit up.

Immediately, a small figure emerged from the floor with some toy cars. Simon ran over to my side.

"Good morning, Miss Kiera."

I pulled the surrounding quilt tighter, attempting to hide that I had soiled myself.

"How do you feel?"

"Like I just got kicked by a horse. What happened?"

"That's what I want to know. Grown-ups never tell me anything. Mom said you might've had a heatstroke. Most tourists here get them. She says she's never seen it so bad."

"Heatstroke, huh? All I remember was feeling scorching hot . . . and then smoke, and a wolf, and—"

"You saw him, too?"

It took me aback for a moment. "What do you know about the wolf?"

"Mom told me I was just imagining things when I saw him. I snuck in for some chocolate while Momma was working. The myst poured into the room. He was big, mean and scary, and called me a lot of bad things. He said I shouldn't be able to do magic, and I would never be a magician. Momma never let me back inside. Sometimes, he chases me in my sleep. Momma doesn't believe me."

"That's terrible, Simon."

He nodded. "But now that you're here, she has to believe me," he said as he grinned.

A bell rang downstairs.

"That's lunch. Miss Montague said she'd bring you up some soup when you're feeling better."

"Miss Montague?"

"The fat lady who was here this morning."

I laughed at his candid description of Hazel. Simon raced downstairs to get lunch. I looked around the room. The bed sat parallel to a bay window overlooking the thoroughfare outside. On both sides were tall shelves of nothing but books.

My mind turned over the dream several times.

Who was this wolf? Was he working with the wyrm?

A table and a study were on my side of the room. On the other side was a hallway and staircase to the ground floor. On the nightstand by my side was a laid out fresh change of clothes.

My legs drooped over the edge of the bed. I tried to stand and found myself on my knees. All the strength seemed pulled from my legs. I leaned on the bed as support, limping to the nightstand.

After cleaning myself up, and changing on the bed, I found that no matter what I did Cheryl's clothes just didn't fit me right. They put stress on my tail, forcing it over. It drove me crazy. My fingers pulled and tugged, trying anything to wrench some room for my tail. It was like someone bent my thumb backward.

Then it happened.

I yipped as something stabbed me. I pulled my hand away. A speck of blood ran down my fingernail. I bent my fingers, palms up, and to my surprise, my nails shot out like cat claws. I extended my fingers, and the claws retracted. First the wolf, now this.

My tail continued to ache. I pulled at the seat of the shorts and twitched my claws in and out, trying to understand what was going on. My nails pulled and tore through the denim. My tail sat more naturally. This gave me an idea.

It took some work, but I carved a small-sized hole in the denim and pulled my tail through. I studied my newfound claws. After that first initial break of the skin, retracting them at will was painless. These would prove useful. Maybe these were the hormones Minnie spoke of.

Moments later, Hazel walked up the steps with a bowl of soup. I still lay on the bed, as the strength hadn't yet returned to my legs. My migraine had only mildly subsided.

"How are you feeling, honey?" Hazel asked.

"A little better."

"Oh, thank goodness. You had us worried sick."

Cheryl slowly trudged up the steps with her head hung low. She carried another bowl. "Yeah, that was some heatstroke," she said as her voice cracked.

Another voice called out from down the hall, "You know very well it wasn't heatstroke."

The wooden floor creaked. A pale, wrinkled woman rode in a chair held atop carriage wheels.

She wagged her bony, jagged finger at Cheryl. "I raised you better than to lie."

"Good afternoon, Madame Sophia," Hazel said, doing a small curtsy to the elderly woman.

She batted her hand as if the gesture wasn't worth her time and continued to wheel herself toward me. Her eyes transfixed on me and bulged. Her teeth grinned a gapped yellow smile, and her wheels wobbled toward me. Hazel attempted to wheel her over, but the lady cursed her and smacked one of her hands with the metal cane on her lap.

"Yes, let's see what we have here," she cackled to herself, wheezing as she rolled the wheels forward.

I crawled a little further away on my back as the pug-eyed lady stared me down. An eternity passed as she silently looked me over.

"What's the matter, dearie? Cat got your tongue?" Sophia's voice was thick and raspy as if she were hoarse.

"No, I just—"

"Well, then, say hello, for crying out loud." Sophia smacked her lips together and ran a tongue over her teeth, and her fingers over her chin.

"I never thought I'd see a pureblood with my own eyes. How lucky am I? Or perhaps very unlucky. Only time will tell, yes?"

Hazel turned to Sophia with a raised eyebrow. "A pureblood what?"

"Hasn't that worthless daughter of mine taught you anything?" Sophia roared.

Cheryl rolled her eyes.

"This young lady's a changeling. The purebloods react violently to the myst. Ancients tell of them as keepers of secrets, ancient machina, and the seven deadly evils. Rumors told, they all died years ago. Except this one." She thumped her seat and pointed her cane at me.

"This one's still ticking. Cheryl! Bring me my soup! We have much to discuss," Sophia rasped out over her shoulder.

Cheryl came over, handed her the bowl of soup in her lap, and tried to warn her it was hot, but Sophia refused help. She simply had to do things her way. That's what I liked about her. I remembered her being wily, kind-natured, and bat-shit crazy. To be honest, that's the way I grew to like her, and there's not a thing I would have done to change it.

Sophia twirled her bony finger in the broth before bringing it to her lips.

"It needs salt," she hissed.

"Mother, we talked about this. The doctor says you eat too much salt."

"Whatever. Leave us, you lay about. It's bad enough I'm the breadwinner in this family. We don't need you killing the poor darling with boredom. We never get enough company."

"Probably because everyone knows about how you threatened those boys who vandalized the window."

"I still say they would have made a nice doormat. The fat slug would have plenty of area coverage," Sophia grumbled. "Leave us in peace. We have much to discuss. But first, we feast. Ha! I was a poet and didn't know it."

I'm fully convinced she was a poet at one point. Simon even found a journal of hers, years later, that helped bolster my claim.

"Well, dearie, let's get down to it. Straighten up, dear. It's bad posture to slouch."

I sat up in bed, unsure what this batty old bird would say or do next. Cheryl and Hazel went back downstairs.

"Tell me about yourself," Sophia continued. "It's not every day I get visitors of such stature."

The old lady brought the spoon to her lips and choked in disgust. She pulled from inside of her bra a small glass vial of salt and poured some in the soup. I laughed. Sophia hissed at me not to say a word to Cheryl.

I told her everything—where I lived, what I learned, and, most importantly, the vision.

"Well, dearie, that's quite a tale," Sophia cackled. "There's no doubt about it. Your reaction proves it. You're a pureblood."

"Is that a bad thing?"

At this point, I began to realize maybe Romero was right. Magic was dangerous and not to be trifled with.

Sophia cackled once more. Her face glowed with her toothy grin. The old lady was having a ball.

"'Is it a bad thing,' she asks? Oh boy, that's rich. No, dearie, it's quite normal. It's who you are. You're changing, that's all. Are you familiar with the birds and the bees?"

"No, but that's really not—"

"You see, when a mommy and daddy love each other very much . . ."

Sophia then told me, ad nauseam, the story of the birds and the bees in rhyming couplets.

Goodbye, childhood.

When she finished, her eyes gazed upon me expectantly for my reaction. All I could muster was a polite "thank you."

She doubled over again. "My, you're like a frightened sparrow, little one. I don't bite. Or at least only a little," she cackled again. "What a hoot. Child, I suppose that dream of yours should prove troubling."

"What does it mean?"

"Your guess is as good as mine."

I frowned. Not the answer I was expecting.

"Now, about this wyrm. I would suppose that someone else is a myst-seer around these parts, and a powerful one at that. Cheryl and I are myst-seers. Magic, dearie, is a large part of our lives and what we do. It's our lives and our livelihood—our heritage.

"The myst allows me to see beyond these walls where I'm bound to this chair. I can see the birds chirping and the wind buffeting the branches. I see. I can explore. We used to help the police force, hence the sewer myst grate in the back room. Sadly, not everyone uses our gift for good, and I fear it may have influenced Cheryl. So, come, follow me."

She placed her bowl on the nightstand and handed me her cane. My legs hadn't fully recovered yet. They bent and shook at strange angles. Mostly, it looked like I had to go to the bathroom as I hobbled after her.

Sophia moved very slowly and deliberately. Her bony fingers seemed as if they got caught in the wheel wells easily. She led me down to the last room on the left.

Inside, the room smelled of baby powder and mothballs. A bed took up most of the room. Everything was in floral print. The silk curtains, bedspreads, and even the salmon wallpaper. All the surfaces had doilies on them.

Sophia sat me down on the bed and asked for her cane back. She used it to pull out a small locked jewelry box from under the bed. She pulled out a key to unlock the box. Inside it, a small moonstone ring lay in the bottom.

"This will help with any watchful eyes."

"No, really, there's no need. I can't accept it."

"Do you want it stalking you or not? Watching?"

I took the ring and thanked her.

"Don't worry about it. I have my own." She flashed her ring. "I never even bathe without it. It's my wedding band."

"Why are you helping me?"

"I hate to see a young girl like yourself so frightened."

"Thank you."

She patted my hand. "Don't mention it, dearie. And this will help put that nosiness in its place."

She reached her cane back under the bed and pulled out a briefcase by the handle.

"Now, are you right- or left-handed?"

I replied that I'm right, and she opened the case. Inside lay two long, leather gloves. Rising to the forearm were drawstrings to tighten them, and fine gold-threaded stitching.

"That works perfectly. Simon will get the other when he becomes of age. We have passed these gloves down since before I was a little girl. There's hare pelt in the cuff and unicorn hair in the stitching. It shall make for a strong casting focus."

"But I know nothing about magic."

"It's like mothering, dear. You'll know what to do when the time comes. Follow your gut and use your head. The heart's a tricky one. It's easily led astray."

I hugged her, and she patted my head. I thanked her again, multiple times. Maybe there were some good people in the world.

"You're most welcome. Anything for a lady of legend. Heaven knows that worthless daughter of mine doesn't deserve it."

"Cheryl seems very nice. Maybe you're being a bit too hard on her."

Sophia grunted. All she mustered was a "Maybe."

CHAPTER EIGHTEEN

Oddly enough, Sophia knew nothing of Minnie, but she knew everything about her. We just chalked it up to "word traveling."

The strength returned to my legs. Sophia continued to rant and ramble on about how a "worthless" person like Cheryl couldn't tell heat stroke from a heritage.

Hazel told me to not worry about the pants. The look Cheryl gave me when she saw what I had done to the seat of her pants scornfully agreed. Other than an apology, she kept to herself and kept her head down.. She would turn to look at me, then turn back, shake her head, and walk away. She never said a word unless spoken to.

Romero may have been right about the magic but I remained determined to prove him wrong. I could prove my innocence. There was no need for some mangled vagabond of a man holding me back. I could do this all by myself . . . or so I thought.

I wasn't sure what time it was when I left the shop, but now nothing would hold me back. I had to prove my innocence. I resolved to get to the docks by the end of the day. It was time to prove him wrong. This "farm girl" would make him eat his words.

Seagulls screeched overhead. The salty sea breeze soothed me on the other side of the city. The blue sky stretched endlessly, unadulterated by even the smallest streak of white. The altitude and the sea made for a unique and exquisite experience. Roads brimmed wide and open under the azure canopy. Granite roads marked the way past theaters and atriums, but progressively, the buildings became more rugged as I approached.

I skirted the inside of the city wall and made the rest of my way to the docks. My eyes darted away at the sight of any patrol on the streets. Romero had explained that we didn't have papers for residency so it was likely they could escort us out if stopped—or worse. I kept my head down. Best not to draw too much attention.

I came to the arch—the cornerstone arch. A high granite arch raised out of the city wall, revealing the rich skyline behind it. Two guards stood at attention on both sides.

One stood in cheap leather armor with a saber by his side. A wide-brimmed, dark hat covered his head with a long feather jutting from the top. The leather and patches on his armor were the only sign of his position.

The other stood in full gleaming plate, with a flowing crimson cape adorned from his shoulders. Unlike the first guard, a helmet covered his face.

The feather-capped guard approached first. "Hold it. Let's see some papers, please."

I stumbled over my words. Eventually, I got out that I didn't have the papers.

"No passage through without a writ of transit or seafarer license. Now step aside."

"Please," I begged, "I need to get through. It's urgent."

"I don't care. No papers, no entry. Step aside."

The plate mail guard stepped in. His voice was gentle, even though his exterior was intimidating.

"Miss, if it is urgent as you say, you can seek a waiver at city hall."

"Don't tell her that. You bloody imperials are enough trouble as it is, visiting. I don't need more beasts stinking up the place around here."

"You best watch your tone. Don't forget who you are talking to."

The feather-capped guard grumbled. "Right. Look, miss be back by nightfall. Gates close by then. Capiche?"

I thanked them and raced off.

The sun began to set in multicolored hues. City hall sat on the other side of town. It towered in the center with a green-domed roof. You couldn't miss it.

As I ran, lights lit one by one, strand by strand. The sky was now a pink streak on the horizon. The sun barely lay in sight. I climbed the stone stairs. Three sets rose up the front door. I wheezed at the top. I yanked on the door. Nothing. I pulled harder. Locked.

I pulled on it several times more, begging it to open, but it was no use. I kicked the door.

All around me, more and more lights turned on. The entire city blossomed with its mysterious energy. The sun sank behind the clouds over the wall, and my heart sank with it.

I plopped down on the stairs.

Romero had been right on both accounts. He'd been right about magic being dangerous, and now he was right about me not being able to do this alone. Now I had heavens-knows-who after me for hell-knows-what. He'd been right about me not being able to do anything by myself.

I refused to believe it. I would march back down there and convince them to let me pass or find my way in myself.

THE SEA BREEZE blew colder at night. I kept a watchful eye over my shoulder. The thought of someone watching me gave me chills. I clutched my ring tight. Shadows rose along the alleyway. I kept walking. A voice called out behind me.

"Hey, you there! Stop where you are."

I didn't turn around. I kept walking and pretended I didn't hear him.

"Hey! Halt!" the voice shouted.

Footsteps raced in with the clangor of metal.

When I turned, patrols were pursuing behind. My legs ran as fast as possible. I was a goner with no papers. They'd boot me out of the city for sure.

I streamed in and out through the crowds on the wide roads. The men pursued, knocking over several denizens. I kept moving and darted into an alleyway. There was no hope in the open. The alleys snaked as the veins of the city.

I laid my back up against the wall. My heart raced. My lungs throbbed. The echoes of footsteps approached closer with shouts. I held my breath. The footfalls echoed down the mouth of the alley. I stood perfectly still. Five patrols raced past the opening. My heart thumped in the back of my throat. After a moment of silence to make sure they left, I finally exhaled.

I let my back slide down the wall and clutched my knees.

What were they after me for? Could they be working for the wolf?

Maybe the ring didn't work. Maybe Sophia was as crazy as she seemed. My chest hurt and my feet ached. I made a promise to myself should I ever get out of this: I would get in shape.

Us pureblood women gotta keep our figures, you know. Gosh, I sound like Romero. That's a scary thought.

When I was ready, I got to my feet. No way I was going back toward the guardhouse gate. I might as well have asked them to arrest me.

I racked my brain for the safest place and set out. How I'd get there was the question.

I stuck to the shadows. The backstreets had treated me well so far. Every girl needs her little black dress—mine was the night sky, and it fit well on many occasions.

Simon's house was too far away. It was best to bed up at Hazel's and try again in the morning. Hopefully, I wouldn't run into Mister Pretty Boy having an I-told-you-so moment.

I continued down the dark street crevices between the buildings. No sound but the echo of my footsteps. The air compressed around me, cold and stagnant. The road rolled a red brick carpet before me. I crossed my arms for warmth. This was not 'shorts weather'. No wonder Cheryl passed them on to me.

The alleys bisected each other in some kind of local labyrinth. As I continued further, I saw a silhouette at one end, blocking the exit. A second joined him and they began talking amongst themselves. There was nowhere to go but back.

I took a step back and hoped they didn't see me. Not looking where I was going, I fell over, crashing down onto a trash can. A loud metal clang echoed. The two shadows stood taller and craned their necks.

"Who goes there?"

Metal armor clinked my way. I scrambled to my feet and sprinted the other way, paying no attention to where I was going. All I knew was that I had to get away. I'd come too far to fail now. There was a fork in the path. My brain fired blanks.

Voices shouted behind me.

"He went this way. Come on."

I went left.

Big mistake. A dead end. Shadows approached. The buildings blocked all light. Two men loomed faceless in the dark.

"You there, what business do you have here at this hour?"

"I . . . I'm j—just on my way home. That's all," I stuttered.

"Right. Papers, please."

"I, um . . ."

Think, Sinopa, think.

"I left them in my other pants."

Good answer.

"A likely story."

Oh gosh, he's not buying it.

"We're on call for a missing person's case. They're wanted in connection to several abductions in the area. Know anything about that?"

I shook my head.

"Hmm. Would you mind stepping into the light? Nice and easy-like," piped the other.

A beam of moonlight shone down on the brickwork. One grabbed a saber at his wrist, ready to draw it as necessary. I took a deep breath, held up my arms, and did as he said.

"Now, pull back your hood. No sudden moves."

It's not like I could go anywhere anyhow. What did he mean, "no sudden moves?" I pulled back the hood of my cloak.

One guard leaned into the other.

"Matches the descriptions to the letter. What do you think?"

"All right, ma'am, we have to bring you in for questioning."

"What?"

I stepped back closer to the wall.

"Don't make this harder than it has to be."

I bolted, trying to run past them, and one caught my arm. I wailed on him with my other.

One guard laughed to the other, "We got a fighter."

"Isn't that cute?" The other guard slapped one manacle around my wrist.

I shrank to the ground, as the guard barely had a hold on my wrist. I clapped the other in the face with my tail, knocking his feather cap clean off. He was out cold on the concrete.

The guard grabbing my wrist, *tsked* at me, and let go. I crawled back away with my shoulders planted against the wall.

"You had to do it the hard way."

He pulled a handkerchief tightly over his face and threw a glass bottle by my ankles. He missed. I got up to run and my world spun. The one conscious guard grabbed my wrist and shushed me. My eyes fluttered. I tried desperately to stay awake. My legs grew limp, and the world faded black.

CHAPTER NINETEEN

I awoke in a wooden chair. Leather straps chafed my wrists and ankles. My prized boots were gone. So was the magic focus gauntlet, my jewelry, and worst of all, the moonstone ring. They had seized anything I had of value: my money, my jewelry, my dignity, and soon much worse—much, much worse.

At this point, I was tired of waking up in strange places. I woke up in less strange places in the goblin village . . . more on that later. I wasn't going down without a fight.

A cold feeling brushed over my body. I wasn't sure from where, but it certainly felt drafty. Metal inlaid plates sat in the wooden chair at my joints, one for each elbow and leg. Copper wires and black cords plugged to the chair by my feet and ran across the room. They stopped under a tarp covering something in the corner.

I sat for what felt like an eternity. Had the chair not been so hard, I probably would have taken another nap.

The room was small. Gray tile encompassed its interior. Various types of what are called "tongue looseners" hung on the wall. A furnace stood against another wall. From what I could tell, a desk and cabinet sat behind me, as if interrogations were just another day at the office or thrown together on the weekends. In front of me was a long glass window showing the guards eating in a mess hall and a row of cells beyond it.

I think they intended to make me sweat a little, but they ended up lulling me to sleep. I awoke sometime later to a bucket of water.

"Wake up!" a voice shouted.

I coughed and shook. Water PTSD had set in again. I couldn't wipe my soaked hair from my eyes.

Two men stood over me, one in finely crafted leather. He was definitely Aerogapolian police. His chin had a clefted goatee, and he reeked of booze. The other stood in dull cadet steel. Emblems in a red silk scarf were wrapped around his neck. The coward's face hid behind his helmet.

"You are to stand trial for your crimes, beast," snapped the goateed man with the bucket.

"I have done nothing wrong. Let me go."

"In due time. I'm the Honorable Judge Cobarde Estaban. This is Grand Protector Heimer of Northstrand, officiating your trial today."

"How is this a fair trial?"

Cobarde laughed.

"In Aerogapolian law, all citizens receive a fair trial. Make no mistake of that, señorita. But, seeing as you have no papers and no way to prove your citizenship, things might get . . . messy."

I swallowed nervously.

"I thought you said it would be a fair trial," said Protector Heimer.

His voice echoed hollow and dark inside his helmet.

Cobarde grinned.

"I shall not convict her. Now, before we begin, release the deserter. We are finished with him."

Heimer's head cocked. I couldn't tell if it was from confusion or from sinister intrigue. He left to do so.

"Now, señorita, let's start, shall we? I'll ask a question, and you answer politely. Don't that sound fun?"

I glared at him and lashed my tail. It was the one thing the kinky freaks didn't tie down.

"You're a changeling, are you not?"

"A what?"

"Don't play dumb with me." He reached forward and grabbed my cheeks. "You're a changeling, are you not?"

I nodded violently.

"Good girl." He tapped my cheek and walked away. He circled me like a vulture. I was dead meat.

"Your kind have lived beside Aerogapolis—well, beneath us really—for generations. We've made peace with you. We've traded with you. And though we've had our differences—and believe me, we have—we've let you coexist. We've even given you land and dominion of the docks as its police and peacekeepers, and the island of Jarbah."

I got the feeling this guy loved to hear himself speak. He blabbed on for minutes.

Heimer returned, escorting from the cell to my right a brown-furred changeling in cuffs. A shiny metal breastplate squeezed his chest with a dent in the front.

"Max?"

He turned and looked at me.

"Kiera? What are you doing here?"

Cobarde sighed.

"Please, sir, you've done your time. Now she must do hers. We are in the middle of a trial."

"Of what charges?"

"Abduction and murder."

"I've been with her all morning. I could be a witness."

"This does not concern you. Go back to your docks and play policeman somewhere else."

Heimer undid his cuffs. Max stole the judge's sword and drew it on him.

"Cobarde, under the order of the Aerogapolian police force, I place you under arrest for fraud, hate crimes, and excessive use of force . . . among other crimes."

Cobarde sighed and snapped his fingers. Heimer drew his sword to Max's neck. Max lowered his weapon.

"Couldn't stay out of trouble, could you, pooch? You saw too much. We were going to let you go, but now you must be punished."

Heimer kicked Max's knees out from under him and cuffed his hands behind his back.

"You wanted to take part in the trial? Fine. You're going to sit and watch like a good boy. Actually, you may even be of use."

I shook my head. "You hurt him, I'll—"

"You'll what?" Heimer raised a sword to Max's throat.

Cobarde continued, "You see, over the past months, several fine and proper folks have gone missing."

And? Just get to the point, you greasy piece of trash, and let me go home.

"Each case was unique, but we believe we have finally cracked what we had suspected all along. Heimer, if you would be so kind."

Max fell over on his side, his ears tucked back. The spurs on Heimer's boots clinked slowly. You could count the even rhythm in his footsteps. A large ebony box with crude steel and copper lines had been revealed under the tarp. A heavy switch jutted out of its side. Next to it was a crate with rowed slots of blue glass marbles. He removed his gauntlet and pulled out a sphere.

It appeared to come to life in his hands. Brass barb-like fingers sprouted. The prickly finger clinked and whined, crying like a hungry infant never satiated.

"Are you aware, beast, what this is?"

Before I could answer he interrupted and leaned in close.

"What am I saying? Of course you're not. Filthy pigs like you aren't worth the air you breathe."

I whipped out my tail, knocking him flat on his rear. Heimer coughed as if he were trying to hold back a laugh.

"I'll give you that, beast. Feisty señorita—I like that. The tougher meat stews better. More . . . juicy."

This guy's a total creep. I whipped my tail out again. It flailed like a viper, warning all who came close. Heimer brought the sphere over in front of me, closer, testing my range. Max whined from the floor.

"This," Cobarde continued, "this is a forget-me-knot. A blue tick. Do you know what we use it for?"

I remained silent, glaring at them. My eyes never left either of them, despite parsing glances at the bug squirming from his fingertips.

"Shame. It's rude not to speak when spoken to. This, my dear, is your ticket out of here. The bug never lies. I guess you'll never know what it does."

Like I cared. Heimer circled behind me. I swung my tail, hoping to strike the buckethead. Buckethead swerved as it panged off his side. I aimed higher. He caught the end in his wrist and twisted. He pulled my tail, hoisting the back of the chair off the ground. My eyes watered in pain. My tail wriggled but remained choked, still.

"Stop! Please. She doesn't know anything," Max begged.

"Is that a confession, pooch?"

"Max, stop," I said.

"I better hear a confession or one of you gets the tick."

"Max, you're going to get yourself hurt."

"If it means protecting you . . . I'll do it. It's my job as a policeman, and I . . . I think I like you, Kiera."

Cobarde rolled his eyes.

"I think I'm going to be sick." He nailed Max in the gut with his boot.

"You monsters make me sick. Heimer, take him away before I vomit."

He released my tail and walked over to Max, who whimpered and cried on the floor.

"You're lucky I don't fix the mutt right here, right now. I wouldn't leave a trace of him—not even a memory. Tell the chief he died by her hand. Send a flag and condolence letter to his family. Empty him of everything he knows. If she doesn't cooperate, burn the corpse when you're done."

Heimer pulled him by his feet. Max whined and cried.

"Remember me, Kiera. Don't let them win."

The door shut.

"You monster!" I screamed.

"Me? No. You filthy, disgusting lot are the monsters."

He stepped closer and I lashed my tail. I had to fight. I had to free Max.

"You want your friend to live, don't you?"

I glared at him and lowered my tail. He grabbed it like before and forced my neck up to look at the wriggling tick.

"And to think I really hired that bounty hunter, Valkyrie, for the library. All I needed was that wimpy little pooch to get to you. By the way, the wyrm queen sends her greetings."

I couldn't believe it. The police chief was tied to the cult snake. My neck craned up at him. The judge grinned over me. The bug squealed and drummed its fingers, hungry.

"Now, señorita, here's the showstopper. Where are they?"

The bug fell. It descended straight, like a drop of water. Its teeth crunched as it bit into my neck. The fingers hummed and massaged. It vibrated and tingled my skin. Jolts shot down my spine. Strangely enough, after the initial prick, it didn't hurt.

In fact, it was almost soothing. Cobarde dropped me upright. My tail slumped to the floor, all feeling in it—gone. Come to think of it, there was no feeling in any part of my body, really. The tick had paralyzed me. Like in a dream, I couldn't move. I'd say that's the best way to describe it.

Time passed slowly. I sat there emotionless, just sucking everything in. No thoughts or opinions. Everything rolled out in a stream of consciousness.

Cobarde riddled me with questions. I couldn't answer any of them, no matter if I wanted to or not. He fed each one to get me to think, feel, and remember my experiences. They loaded some questions to incriminate, and others made Heimer and Cobarde seem loving. They were gods to me. Every word of theirs was truth to me even if it was ridiculous or irrational.

I don't know how long I was under the forget-me-knot. I remember hearing it hiss, and I felt steam from the back of my neck. Cobarde removed it. White, cloudy juice stirred inside the blue crystal glass.

I yawned. Drowsiness was a side effect of the forget-me-knot, among other things.

Cobarde taunted me, saying something about the evidence they had gathered, but the verdict was still out. They needed it—"testimony," as he put it. Heimer looked away. He stood there, still and tall, with his back to me and head hung low. I was brought to the stand as he placed his hand on the large trap switch from the grotesque wired box. My breathing sped up. My head shook.

I'll spare you the details for the sake of children in the room, but, needless to say, it wasn't pretty. I confessed to anything and everything. Blue-colored current and foggy mist clouded my body. My throat burned. The rest of me chilled ice cold as if it were drafty again. If I tried to resist one way, the metal plates somewhere else zapped me from radiating jolts.

I heard a voice, the same voice of the wolf from before.

"Hang tight, my sweet kitten. I'm coming soon. Yes, I'm coming soon. We shall make all wrongs right. Yes, all wrongs shall be made right."

CHAPTER TWENTY

The only strong memory I can vividly recall was waking up.

After I had satisfied the honest and honorable law, they left me alone, still strapped to the chair to await my sentence. Dried blood coated my lips, a pasty thick lip gloss. Iron made up probably half my spit.

My clothes had holes shredded through them. Red marks stained my scaly skin from where the lightning's lips had kissed it. I wanted death more than anything— almost as much as I wanted to beat their faces in. But more than that, I wanted it to be over. Any way possible.

Sweat and blood dripped from my nose icicles in the thaw of spring. The black box had drawn a lot of heat into the room. Static pulsed from the plates.

My bones ached, my head throbbed, and I hadn't drunk anything in hours. I was alive, but barely. Despite everything I'd been through, I was a survivor. I remained victorious. They couldn't take that from me.

Out the long window, a sparse couple of tipsy guards partied into the graveyard shift. No doubt slimy Goat Face and pompous Buckethead were out there bragging right now.

In an instant, the music died. I was too tired to even raise my head to look. There were shouts, and several guards shot out of the dining hall.

Three remained: Cobarde, Heimer, and a third in shining plate mail. A cape of red fabric flowed from his shoulders.

"Give me the keys," one shouted.

The caped man swung open the metal door, clanging into the wall.

"Master, you understand that we followed all the protocol prescribed," whined Cobarde.

"Give me the knot!" he roared.

"Let's not be hasty," argued Heimer.

"Give me the knot. Don't make me ask again."

I can only assume Heimer gave it to him. I only saw their ankles. My breathing was slow and heavy. The ankles came closer until I stared blankly at the breastplate of the caped man. All fear, bitterness, and malice had left. I accepted my fate, whatever it was. He tilted up my chin. I looked expressionlessly into his helmet. I attempted to lift my tail, but it only fell back where it lay.

"She's got the spark. This better have been worth it," he mumbled.

I summoned the strength to hold my head upright. He held the knot up to my eyes. Pictures flashed within the knot. It showed Cobarde berating me and bullying me for answers. It showed Heimer standing by, letting it happen.

It showed them as they really were—pathetic. A few images seemed familiar, like I had experienced them before. Then it all came back to me. Goat Face had asked where I was at the time of one of the disappearances. The knot flashed images of me playing with Simon through my eyes. The blue tick had sucked my memories, and it spat them back with a vengeance.

"You spilled innocent blood," said the man in the cape. His voice remained stern and calm. Was this a caped crusader of villainy, or my knight in shining armor?

"You're unfamiliar with Aerogapolian law, Señor Master. These fiends seek to destroy our way of life."

"Enough. Get out of my sight. The consul shall hear of this, I assure you. And you," he said, this time referring to Heimer, "I expected better of you."

Cobarde grumbled, passing the blame onto Heimer on the way out.

My head slumped again and I stared at my knees. A helmet jumped into my lap. Horrifying thoughts jostled me to life at that. I raised my tail weakly and swatted at him.

"Please, let me help you."

The caped guard removed his gloves and tossed them to the ground. His fat hands lifted my chin up to look him in the eye. They glowed a clear blue as if a brook of water ran through them. His helmet hair buckled in a different direction, the color of coarse straw. Stubble lined his cheeks.

I swatted him in the face, but in my current state, it was only as if I had dragged it across his face, brushing his hair away from it. He placed his fingers around my freshly blackened eyes.

A stirring heat ran through his fingertips. It didn't burn but felt hot to the touch. Then it vibrated cold and soothing like flowing water. I could feel my bruise vanish, my cuts mend, and the dried blood crumble away.

He did it again several times until all the burns from the black box vanished. My muscles even felt refreshed. I could run laps. Hopefully, now, I could run away from all of this. He slowly undid the straps and helped me to my feet.

He placed his arm out for me for balance. I wearily took it but fell to my knees on the floor.

In a small box behind the desk were my belongings, even the moon-stone ring. I happily slipped it on, and the gauntlet, too. He took his helmet and carried it under his other arm.

"How do you feel?" he asked.

"Better, thank you."

I recognized his voice now. This was the same guard from the gate who had told me about the waiver at the city hall.

"People around here don't know how to treat others with respect," he said.

I nodded.

My thoughts turned fuzzily to a brown-furred man. His howls echoed in my mind.

"My friend. They took him in there." I said, pointing toward the door.

He went out and shut the door behind him.

Memories and feelings slowly started washing over me, but they were disconnected. My mind struggled to form complete thoughts.

I'm not sure how long he was gone. I jumped at the sound of the door shutting behind him when he entered. He stooped down to my level.

"Is he . . . ?" I couldn't think of the word.

"He's alive, but only just. He'll be lucky to make it through the night —even luckier if he has any wits to him—but I swear on my honor that I'll do everything I can to save him."

I nodded. I had no thoughts or feelings to express.

Who is this stranger I care about?

The man in armor helped me outside. The crickets chirped and the air loomed thick with dew. Daybreak would be soon.

"Where are you staying?" he asked.

I replied that I wasn't sure. Details hadn't entirely returned, but memories were slowly coming back. The man suggested a place that felt familiar and I agreed.

I rested my head on his arm. He seemed to take no notice. Men in leather stopped in salute as he walked by. He nodded in acknowledgement and continued, never speeding up or slowing down, but gently leading me on.

His touch pulled gentle and strong. My tail gently bobbed to and fro on our little stroll on air to Hazel's Parlor and Inn. The sun dawned as we ascended the stairs. It was about time I met a true gentleman.

Inside, a plump lady, whom I felt oddly eager to see, stood arguing with an equally familiar, gruff man in a long jacket.

"No, and I keep telling you I haven't seen her. The last I saw her she —" Hazel told the man before locking eyes with me.

The gruff man turned and walked away at the sight of a lawman coming in.

"Room for one, please," the armored man said. "And make sure you take good care of this one. You'll be compensated in full." He tossed a hefty coin purse onto the counter. He eased me onto a stool.

The lady's eyes bulged.

"Yes, sir. Right away, sir."

The man patted me on the shoulder.

"Till we meet again. Know that you are always welcome in Northstrand and our estate off the docks. Just say my name. That should be enough. Tell 'em High Master Rudolph sent you. For now, get some rest. You'll feel better soon."

I propped my head on my fist at the bar. As I watched him leave, the wind brought up the end of his flowing cape and I sighed. My tail wagged back and forth, gently flicking up at the tip like a campfire crackling in the wind.

Hazel muttered to herself, "The girl comes in with a ragamuffin stray and leaves with the prince, and a sack of gold to boot. Atta girl. Get back on the horse. Sign me up for the next one."

CHAPTER TWENTY-ONE

M aster Rudolph was right. I needed that sleep. I felt renewed. Gone was the pain and shame of yesterday. My body had healed, and it restored my memories. As I rolled over, my tail still flicked and fluttered at the thought of the high master.

Who is this strange man that he would care for me? How can I see him again?

My heart practically purred with daydreaming about him. *Goodbye, Romero. You had your chance. Hello, sweet prince.* I didn't even know what a master was.

I rolled over to look toward the window. This room was much nicer than the one I slept in my first night. There were beautiful white silk curtains around the window. All the furniture matched in a rich, dark walnut wood. Come to think of it, I didn't remember going to bed. That's how messed up I was. No, I had Hazel to thank for getting me to my room.

There was a soft knock at the door. I slipped out of the covers. My clothes were still the same—covered in holes. I opened the door and Hazel stood there expectantly.

"You feeling all right, dearie? It's past noon. You've slept a good twelve hours."

I embraced her tight, squeezing my arms around her. She jumped, surprised, and patted my head.

"There, there, child. Everything will be all right."

"Oh, Hazel, it was wonderful. I met someone."

"He wouldn't have been a moth, would he? Your clothes look terrible, and you just got them yesterday."

"Sorry, but—"

"Don't apologize to me. Those are Cheryl's clothes, not mine."

"Yes, but oh! Hazel, he was wonderful."

"I met him last night, dearie. Quite the catch angling yourself a master of high law."

"Hazel, what's a master, anyway?"

"Well, to be honest, I don't know. They're supposed to be guardians of some kind. Better ask him yourself."

"How can I get him to like me?"

"Oh, pish-posh. Just be yourself and you'll be fine. He sent two men to check in on you. They paid well, too. By all means, if it brings me more coin, do it."

"But what if he doesn't? In case you haven't noticed," I flicked one of my horns, "I'm not the most attractive belle of the ball."

"Why should it bother you whether he likes you or not? Take it from me, don't put your worth in someone else's hands. You'll be disappointed. Go ask him yourself. If he does, great. If he doesn't, it's his loss. Now, come downstairs; your breakfast's getting cold. Someone left you a change of clothes."

By someone, I could only assume she meant Romero. Sadly, I still hadn't held up my end of the bargain. Turns out, all morning, he'd been pestering Hazel to see me.

I went downstairs and a bowl of porridge and toast were laid before me. Not my favorite, but free food is free food.

Not to mention I was absolutely starving. I stuffed my face voraciously. Hazel gave a nod of approval, handing me a napkin. She mumbled under her breath that at least somebody liked her cooking. Out of the corner of my eye, someone sat down beside me.

"I won't hear a word about you pestering this girl," snapped Hazel.

I looked up and Romero sat smirking at me. His long, button coat hung open to reveal a prim and proper dress shirt with a ruffled collar.

"You try anything funny," Hazel continued, "and I'll get the guard faster than you can say—"

"It's all right, Hazel. I got this," I said.

Hazel hovered nearby, wiping down the same spot repeatedly on the corner of the bar. Her eyes occasionally wandered over.

"What do you want?" I asked Romero, returning to my plate.

I wouldn't even look him in the eye.

"What do I want? I want to know where you've been. Do you have any idea the trouble I went through?"

"Trouble *you* went through?!" I slammed my spoon down on the counter. "Do you have any idea where I've been?"

"No. Why do you think I've hung around here so long? They could be halfway gone by now."

Hazel came over and grabbed my plate.

"Cool it, both of you! I won't have you scaring away my customers."

I glance around at the empty, late-midday bar.

As Hazel left, I spoke through pursed lips, gritting my teeth.

"You want to know? Fine. I'll tell you. I had been doing everything all by myself. And guess what? I made more headway without you. I've found lots—no, loads—by myself. Not only that, but I've found out who I am. Turns out I'm a sorceress and a pureblood changeling."

"Hey, keep it down!" Hazel shouted from the kitchen.

Romero rolled his eyes.

"Shocker," he said, unimpressed.

"Wait, you knew? And you didn't tell me?"

"Why d'you think I even took you along? Nobody sees a four-foot-two, fully-scaled creature with the spark in her eye without fear."

"I'm a solid five feet," I snapped.

"Whatever, princess. You'll be more than capable—with my help, of course. That is, if you even want the job?"

I hated him calling me that.

"What else are you hiding from me? What else do you know?" I asked.

Romero laughed.

"It's like looking in a mirror. What do you want to know?"

"Who are you really?" I plied him.

"Wouldn't you like to know? Hazel, what's a man gotta do to get a drink around here?"

Hazel came over, poured him a glass, and took the money he set on the counter.

"Thanks, doll."

Hazel mumbled to herself how, unless she was getting paid money, he should get out of her sight. Romero grinned wide. He seemed to enjoy torturing the poor woman.

"Now, where were we?" he asked me.

"You were about to tell me who you really are."

"Sorry, kid. That's a personal question, and I don't answer those," he said, tilting back the tankard. "Now, are you going to help after all or not?"

"Why should I?"

"Didn't you read the note?"

I hadn't. I pulled it from my cloak still in the envelope. The paper had all but deteriorated in a soggy, pasted wad.

"Well, while you were partying it up and reaping what you had sown, no doubt, I was fetching these."

He pulled from his coat pocket two folded vellum documents.

"These should help you get around the city much easier."

"You got us papers?"

"Forged them, really."

"How?"

"A man of my stature has his ways. The black market truly is a booming blessing nowadays."

All this time, if I had just stayed put, I would have been fine. I wouldn't have been hunted. I wouldn't have been arrested. My blood boiled.

"Why didn't you tell me?"

His hands snatched the letter from mine and waved it in my face. I snatched it back, nearly ripping it in half. I hated myself. There was no one else to blame.

"I'm sorry," I murmured.

"Apology accepted. Now, I've brought you here. Can I expect you to hold up your end of the bargain?"

I nodded.

"Splendid. Now I have an errand to run. Meet you by the docks at, say, sunset?"

I agreed. He patted me on the back.

"Great. Eat up, princess. You're gonna need it."

My head began to feel about as mushy as Hazel's porridge. I guess he cared. But I still couldn't trust him.

What is he hiding?

❧

THERE WERE STILL a few hours till dusk. I gorged myself at Hazel's as much as I could. After Romeo left, she pulled up a plate and sat down beside me.

"How are you holding up, love?"

"Confused."

I twirled my fork in figure eights across the plate, lost in thought.

"That'll happen. Don't let that one in your head. He'll toy with you and hijack your noggin."

He wouldn't be the first.

Hazel offered me one of her biscuits and I politely refused.

"Kiera, love, I couldn't help but overhear, and there's something I feel worth mentioning."

We both knew she could have butted out. She just chose not to.

"Cheryl doesn't normally feel comfortable on this topic. It hits too close to home, so I feel the need to take it upon myself. You mentioned you were a sorceress to Romero rather openly, and I just want you to be more careful. Magic may be legal here, but not everyone takes to it too well. Wars raged over it and the old way of life. People fought and died, refusing to budge either way. While lynching hasn't happened here, thank goodness . . . just be careful."

"Sorry."

"No need to apologize. You have a gift."

"Or a curse."

Hazel slapped me with her spoon.

"What was that for?"

"No negative self-talk. You have a gift. I wish I had half the gift you have. I'll be more than happy to take you to Sophia if you wish. Our people have a duty to take care of each other."

"Seems like Romero knew what I was in a heartbeat."

"It takes a trained eye to see the glimmer, but Old Slim is something else. I was way past glimmer age when he found me. He's brainier than he lets on, that's for sure."

I asked her how much she knew about who Romero really was. Best she could tell, he was from Northstrand, by his accent, and wasn't very fond of government, but beyond that she was just as clueless as I was.

ɸ❀

WE WENT to Sophia's after breakfast, which was an early dinner. Simon let us in. He proudly boasted how he'd been running the shop all day by himself. Cheryl hadn't been at home all day.

Apparently, she blamed herself for my accident and had acted more reserved ever since. Hazel remarked how unusual it was for Cheryl to leave without explanation. The shelves were getting sparse, so it was likely she had gone out to get supplies.

Hazel, always the cook, made Simon dinner as he hadn't eaten all day, either. I went upstairs to check on Sophia. As I reached the top step, I nearly slipped on a loose paper.

Inside the library upstairs, books appeared flung across the room. Towers of them lined the hallway. Someone had scattered papers every- where. A few overturned jars of ink dripped over the edge of the desk. The bed by the window glowed white, stripped bare.

I crept down the hall and knocked on the door. The sound of papers crumbling and a heavy book slamming shut echoed inside.

"Sophia?"

I cracked open the door and a bolt whizzed by my ear. The shaft stuck into the door frame by my head. The old lady sat in her chair, tightly holding her crossbow in her lap. Books sprawled everywhere across the floor.

"Don't scare me like that, dearie," she said, lowering the crossbow.

"What was that for? You could have killed me."

"Thank goodness you're here. You can help us pack."

I placed a hand over my chest, my heart still beating wildly.

"Well, don't just stand there. Get a move on, lazy bones. They could be here any minute."

"Whoa, slow down, Sophia. You're not making any sense."

"We don't have time, Kiera. Step aside so I can get my books."

"Who? Who? Who is coming?"

"My gosh, you sound like an owl. We don't have time for this. I could place a ward over the store just in case, but I'll feel much safer away from here. Grab Simon's glove under the bed, will you?"

I did as she said and tried to catch up with the elderly woman wheeling down the hall.

She raced off, pulling books off the shelves and scribbling ink into a leather-bound journal.

"I see through the myst, and this time I saw too much. Darn blasted quill. Hand me the other one on the desk."

I reached for the black turkey feather. Ink dripped onto my hands. I tried to wipe some on my pants before handing it to her.

"Never mind the ink."

"What are you doing?"

"Preparing spells. What else?"

"I thought you said magic comes from within."

"I did. These books—stories, poetry, and history—they make up the lifeblood of our conditions. They capture our experiences and our emotions. Magic is a talent that requires as much feeling as it does intellect or skill. Why else would I tell you to guard your heart? Everything you do flows from it, and it is the most wicked organ next to the tongue."

"So you're writing the words for the feelings?"

"Precisely. There are no magic words like the enrapturement of stories, songs, and poetry. Rage and anger for destruction. Heartbreak and gloom boost better weather charms. I don't have time to get into the details. We're running out of time. Slip this one in the pack behind the chair, will you?"

She handed me a worn leather book with flaking gold trim and began copying another. I flipped through the yellowed pages. The red and black ink had all but faded in spots.

"Sorry, Sophia, but I still don't understand. Who's after you?"

"It's not who's after me. It's who *might* be after me. I was searching for Cheryl through my myst and I saw them.

"Their bodies stood in various forms and sizes. They were changelings, dear. And worst of all, I found Cheryl. She lay in the alley upside down. Her body was overgrown with thorns. They put a large sack over her head and out of my range. Before they left, one stopped. It turned and looked blankly. It stared me down, dead in the eye. They saw me. My ring had shattered, and I hadn't caught it before scrying through my crystal ball."

"That's terrible. Wait, you saw what they looked like? Why didn't you go to the police?"

Sophia fumbled with the book in her hands. "A letter came to the house this morning." She pulled it from inside her blouse and handed it to me.

To whom it may concern,

Cheryl Samarie will henceforth be under the care of the Order of the Archaeopteryx. If you know what is best for her, you shall release to the Order the pureblood. We know you have her. We shall release our servant for the one kitten lost from the litter. Failure to do so could and/or will cause your and Miss Samarie's immediate demise. Speak to the guard and her end shall be long and painful.

We are watching. Our eyes and ears are open, and we are clawing at

your door. Beware, this is your one and final warning. We hope we can
spare her life and yours before nightfall. Unlike your kind.
Sincerely, Mammon Fenrir
P.S. All hail the High Wolf. All hail the Order.

They'd stamped a paw print sealed in blood to the bottom of the
letter.

"They sent proof, too. Even removed the moonstone from her ring
finger."

Her whole finger? I gagged and refused to hold the envelope any
longer.

"They have my baby, Kiera. They have my baby, and I don't know
what to do," Sophia wept.

A small gray storm cloud condensed, sprinkling inside the study. I
knelt and held her hand, squeezing her bony fingers.

"I'm sorry, Sophia."

"Now you understand what I must do."

"What? No, I don't understand," I said.

"I'm out of time. I'm so sorry, Kiera."

My eyes turned to my hand. Thorns snaked up from her chair,
choking my wrist.

"She's here! She's here! Do you hear that, you filthy animals? She's
here." Sophia blew a dog whistle covered in flakes of dried blood around
her neck.

With every pull, the thorns tightened and enlarged on my entangled
wrist.

Sophia wept harder, watching me struggle, and the rain poured
harder.

"Let me go. I can help you," I said. "We can figure something out."

The vine constricted again.

"Don't make this harder on me. They have my baby. I like you,
Kiera. I do. Don't make this harder on me." She blew the silent whistle
again.

"She's here! She's here! Can't you hear me?"

I tugged at the vines. They climbed up my other arm and grew faster as the rain poured into the study. I pulled again. Her chair tilted toward me on one wheel.

"Dang you, worthless fiends. Bring her back. She's here. She's here!"

I pulled again.

The vines snapped. Sophia's chair came down and tilted on the other side before banging on the hardwood floor.

Hazel raced up the steps due to the commotion. The thorns withered and shrank back into the wood from where they had sprung. The pitch-colored cloud thundered and gushed.

All the papers flushed into mounds of gray and white. The wooden wheelchair lay toppled. Its wheels spun.

Sophia balled up on the floor and sobbed. Her white wisps of hair had matted, soaked, to her scalp and forehead. She lay there sobbing, pleading how it wasn't her fault. To me or herself, I may never know. A small scarlet puddle formed around her temple and mixed with the pasty slush, and in the study's stillness, she found a brief moment of peace.

CHAPTER TWENTY-TWO

Hazel tended to Sophia while I took Simon to the inn to stay. There was no sticking around any longer, just in case she tried anything funny. I felt sorry for Sophia. I felt sorry for Simon having the possibility of living without a mother or grandmother. I was sorry for Cheryl that she must endure all this, and all because of me. It was my fault.

Simon remained oblivious to it all. He skipped around, just happy to have a friend, and eager to play and do anything. He twirled about in the street and danced, having a grand old time. I stayed and played with him at the inn until Hazel arrived. We tried more magic lessons but to no avail. It wouldn't work no matter how much I tried to lift those little ball bearings.

He'd console me, "Momma will be happy to teach you when she comes home."

I didn't correct him. Hazel never returned with Sophia. Sadly, much like her, I was out of time. I rushed off across town to meet Romero, as planned, by the gate. True to form, Mister Pretty Boy was nowhere in sight. Typical.

The sunset burned the brick and sandstone into a wall of orange-like glowing fire. Even the granite turned richer hues. The streetlights came on one by one as the crickets commenced their joyous chorus.

I was getting impatient. Then, in the stillness, a whistle called from behind me. I turned to see Romero in an alley, calling me closer.

"There you are! Where have you been? You said sunset!" I exclaimed.

He put his finger to his lips, shushing me.

"Keep it down, will you? There's been a change in plans. Here, take this."

He handed me a long black-sheathed saber. The handle curved around with a polished steel guard engraved in an ornate spiderweb pattern.

"Where did you get that? I thought weapons are illegal in the city."

"Not without the proper paperwork they aren't. Consider it yours. Weapons permits are too pricey for me. Just another perk for being a changeling, I suppose."

I fought to attach the sheath to my side like a toddler trying helplessly to tie his shoes. Romero pulled the belt tight around my waist, pinching my skin.

"Great. Now we're ready to go." He handed me my papers. "Now, remember, stick to your story. You're Kiera Cartwright, a hired handmaiden seeking asylum and citizenship."

"So, I'm supposed to be your slave?"

"Handmaiden, Kiera. *Handmaiden.* You have rights. Our business here is seeking my betrothed, who hired you and whom you didn't know well. That should cover most of the bases. You think you can remember all that?"

Truth be told, I remained stuck on whether I was really some kind of slave. "I think so."

"I suppose it will have to do."

"What if I'm not sure or I mess up? I've never pretended to be someone else before."

"Then improvise. You're the leading lady, aren't you? I wouldn't cast someone I didn't think was fit for the part."

My eyes rolled. I tugged at the belt, pulling at my scales to loosen it. My pudgy baby fat—and yes, it was baby fat, I assure you—bulged over the belt on both sides. You can have baby fat at seventeen, right?

I pulled the saber from the sheath. The steel blade glistened in the moonlight.

"Careful. That's a weapon, not a toy, understood? So, don't just go swinging it around or brandishing it like you're homicidal."

I made a few swipes at the surrounding air before plunging it forward in a stabbing motion.

"How was that?"

His face was unamused.

"Perfect, if you were in a pop-up book. This is the real world, kid. People don't fight with flashy stage flair. They fight to stay alive. Your form is sloppy and your stance is all wrong. If it had been a real fight, you would have been dead in a matter of seconds."

I proceeded to tell him off, saying he didn't know a single thing he was talking about.

"Whatever. Put it away, killer; we're burning moonlight. Remember the fireworks the night before?"

"Yes, they were lovely. Why?"

"Well, we missed the parade, but that was a welcome wagon for the consul visiting Aerogapolis. That's why the security is so tight. Everyone's on edge. Some of the world's most powerful men are all meeting in the same place. Our target should stay with the consul and representatives from Northstrand."

"Your girlfriend's that high up, is she?"

"Only the best for a man of my stature."

"So how are we supposed to even get near her?"

"We don't. We take one step closer, survey the chessboard, and decide our next move. Ready?"

He held out his hand out for me. I thought he wanted to shake on it. My fingers weakly grasped his hand, and he pulled me along like a helpless child. I thumped him one good, and he released me, laughing.

Two guards stood watch at the cornerstone gate like last time. Only this time a different Northstrand soldier stood watch in place of Master Rudolph. To my dismay, there was no cape of flashy symbols.

"You, there. Stop where you are. Gates close after—" He stopped midsentence because he recognized me. It was the same feather-capped guard as before. "You again? All right, let her through."

To my surprise, the man in armor began patting me down. When he patted at my breast pocket, I slapped his hand away.

"What are you hiding there?" he snapped.

I crossed my arms, feeling violated.

"You're a pervert, you know that?"

He pulled from my inside breast pocket the folded vellum papers, and I screamed.

"All right, free to pass. Next!"

I took back the papers and defiantly flashed them in the feather cap's face.

He grumbled under his breath, "Filthy creatures always get their way."

A smug grin crept across my face as I stood with my back to the wall. I had done it—I'd finally gotten past the gate.

Romero approached next, flashing his papers. The armored guard patted him down. He stopped at a few bulges.

"Sir, I will need you to empty your pockets."

Romero stripped down, throwing several small pouches on the ground. At the sight of a knife the guard grabbed him by the collar.

"No blades longer than three inches without a weapons permit."

"Pity. I just so happen to have both the hunting and fishing stipulations that claim otherwise in my back pocket."

The guard roared. "Are you telling me how to do my job?"

The feather-capped guard interjected. "Just continue on, man. My feet are killing me. Let it go."

The man finished his search, inspecting every pouch and doing a second pat-down. This time the search uncovered the flintlocks.

"And just what do we have here?"

"Hmm, looks to me like a high-class instrument of some sort. Something you would know nothing about," Romero said.

"What did you say?" snapped the guard.

"He didn't mean it," I butted in. *What is he doing? Is he trying to get us thrown in prison?*

"Looks to me like a weapon," spat the guard from inside his helmet.

"Chauncey, just let them pass. We don't get paid enough to care as it is."

"Sorry. I can't let him pass."

"It's okay. He's with me." I flashed my papers, including the weapons pass.

The armored man snarled in my face, "If I hear one sign of trouble, I'll have both your heads. You got that, lass?"

I nodded.

"Good. Now beat it."

Romero gathered his things and straightened out his collar. He tucked his fingers on the inside flaps of his jacket with his elbows out, strolling past them like some pompous idiot. "Enjoy the rest of your night."

As we walked away, we could hear the guard shouting in the distance, "What's that supposed to mean? Come back here and say it to my face!"

Romero proudly smiled in triumph over them. I shook my head at him, smiling. He took my arm and began down the wooden pier in the salt-filled air.

☙

THE SILVERY MOON glistened over the ocean, reflecting a rippled path across the waves. It was alive. For now, it was alive. With every breath it proved it. With every pull of the waves, it inhaled the sea-foam curls back, holding them, stilling frothy foamed fingers for a moment, then it exhaled.

The moon mourned. It stretched forward across the beach, reaching and calling, and rose alone in the burnt gray expanse. It lay smothered in a bed of clouds. Its cotton-colored callous rose on the beach, pounding, sliding up the shore as far as they could. At its peak, it would sigh. Then the fingers clawed the sand, desperately digging the dunes for a finger-hold. There were none. The moon breathed all night long. They were slow, deep, mourning breaths.

These were my thoughts as I stood on the pier, overlooking the beach with Romero. We had the same moon before us. I wondered if he saw it as I did.

Even in all its loneliness, the moon glowed in a beauty all its own. In her own hour, away from the sun and bustling of man, she rose in her silvery, misty-blue beauty and called for a friend. I felt empowered somehow that she could desire someone like me.

"Yep, the tides are right, Kiera. We're going to do this," Romero said, finally breaking the silence. "That's the salty taste of victory."

His footfalls creaked along the boards. His emerald eyes shimmered in the light. We strolled along the pier to the port. I knew this section of the city as Puerto del Jerbal or Jarbah Port, depending on who was telling the story.

Jarbah is the entire archipelago off the coast, so whoever's naming these things really deserves to be fired. Perspective is everything, I suppose.

It was a beautiful place. The cactus buds sprouted, flowering from the crags of the cliff. It was just like Clyde had said. Olive, pomegranate, and the rare plum tree curled out of what little sandy soil they had toward the sun. Joshua trees lined the beach, grown bent over from the wind. I considered it lovely how, despite all the wind and tempests, they had endured; the trees grew up stronger and more beautiful than the rest. Thin, prissy palm trees didn't last very long around here.

As we approached the end of the wooden walkway, two figures stood at attention.

"Halt. Who goes there?" a voice barked as we approached.

They were both in uniform—not much armor, per se, save a rusted metal breastplate. One looked oddly familiar. His German Shepherd face puffed in fluffy fur, his body in the form of a man. The other stood in the form of a man with dark chocolate skin smoothly silhouetted against the rock.

"Take it easy, Max. You two, no one's supposed to be up here. State your name and business."

The name rang a bell, an extremely faint bell.

Romero stepped forward into the man's face.

"We are here on personal business to see Jasper himself."

The guard choked in his throat.

"Oh, and I'm Kiera," I piped in, trying to help.

They all turned and shot me a strange look.

"I like your eyes," Max said, panting.

"Um, thanks?"

It did nothing to make the situation any less awkward. Max's voice was low and gravelly. His demeanor was quirky as if he were delirious and lacked common sense. His tone seemed to fluctuate like howling one moment, then rang true in gritty barks the next. Again, it caught me wildly off guard.

The human guard stepped aside at the name of Jasper.

"Right this way. Sorry to keep you waiting."

"Bye, Kiera," barked Max.

"Bye, Max," I said.

Their voices bounced off the cliffs as we descended the steps. "That girl was a real cutie," said the man. An echoing howl came from Max in agreement.

My cheeks blushed a darker shade of red. I walked with a little strut and swagger in my hips. I twirled my tail around like a lasso, and Romero rolled his eyes.

Sometimes you just gotta flaunt what you got. In the words of the ancients, shake what your mama gave you . . . whatever that means.

For once in my life, I'm beautiful. For once, I could fit in here. They accept me. I could get used to this.

If magic pulls on emotions, as Sophia said, I wondered what kind this was. Elation poured over me. I felt a bubbly sensation in my chest, as if there were a constricting knot inside, and I liked it. I felt so happy for once and walked on air. Not literally, but I felt I could. If it was true, this was the magic of flight. No doubt about it.

A strange sensation of relief washed over me after seeing the familiar dog man. It overjoyed me. I topped it off to wanting more compliments. This red bombshell was ready to hit the streets. I had to prove my innocence, sure, but nobody said I couldn't break a few hearts while I was at it.

We continued. The pier descended the slate mountain in a zigzag of wooden struts connected by staircases. It appeared as if someone had etched it in the mountain like a zipper. They carved houses into the sides of the cliffs. Electricity ran there, too. The lanterns had smooth white bulbs as opposed to the normal rectangular, hooded ones. They were like little twinkling stars along the beach.

People here were different. There were changelings everywhere. I had never seen so many. There were wolfish men, lynx-like ladies, even bears and mice. None existed entirely in animal form. There was always only a hint of beast in every person; the rest was as human as everyone else.

It was strange. There were both full humans and changelings. They were laughing, asking after each other's families, and some even held hands as couples. Peace hung in the air. It lived and breathed here. Maybe that's what the moon was reaching for. It's what we were all reaching for: connection.

CHAPTER TWENTY-THREE

The floor rocked beneath my feet. My legs and stomach jostled. I felt as if I would hurl but tried not to. I'd never been on a boat before. With every bump of the waves, my stomach felt more and more uneasy. I tried to enjoy the ride as much as I could.

This was the last ferry to the islands until morning. The ride provided a much better view of the coast. The city towered above the rocks and cliffs. From way down here, one couldn't help but feel insignificant. The massive moon loomed ahead. The vast plateau of ocean waves encroached on us, and the city cliffs beaconed out into the distance.

I clung to the side rails of the boat. The ferry's hull was covered in a darling picket white. The deck glowed with dark cherry wood. It had few passengers that night: a few fishermen returning home to their families, a watchman or two ending their shift, and most of the passengers were couples. They were lovers. Small clusters stood side by side, clutching together or resting on the other's shoulder, gazing out in the sea.

An arm smacked my shoulder.

"Hey, having fun yet?"

I leapt out of my skin and nearly over the guardrail. The waves jostled the deck again, and I lost my footing. That did it. My feet clumsily tried to stand as fast as they could. I stuck my head through the bars and spewed.

"First time?" Romero asked.

I nodded my head between hurls into the ocean.

"Don't worry kid. We're almost there."

He rubbed my shoulders in small circles as I excreted my insides over the railing. Somehow, I think we killed "the moment" for everyone else with that. Nothing's more romantic than vomit, right?

We landed on the shores of Jarbah and I struggled with my sea legs. Two or three giant windmills stood on the island. Lots of foliage and palms lined the beach, unlike where we'd left. It was a jungle outside the village. Lemurs and monkeys screeched in the distance. The sweetness of plantains, mangos, and wet leaves wafted through the trees.

Mossy stones comprised most of the few paved roads beyond the pier. The rest clumped together in a thick, irony clay. It's the kind that stuck like glue when wet and formed red dust clouds when dry.

Again, the small, sleepy town appeared unaffected by the outside world. Both changelings and humans greeted each other on the streets. They wished each other well and engaged in small talk as if they knew each other. I couldn't help but wonder how these same changelings could have taken Cheryl away.

I decided I would bring up the matter to Romero, but I wasn't sure how.

"Everyone here seems so happy. Don't they know what people think of them?"

"Ignorance is bliss."

"What's that supposed to mean?"

"Think about it. I'm sure you'll figure it out."

I'm not sure if he was being genuine or an ass when he put it that way. No good transition came to mind. I decided to just come out with it and tell him about what happened to Cheryl.

"So, what do you think?" I asked.

"It's not our problem."

"What do you mean, 'It's not our problem?' It's all my fault."

"Oh, well. I hired you with one purpose: you're going to help me get our man. Playing hero is outside of my job description. It's not that I don't care. It's that I can't. There are hornets' nests all over this place. And you and that tail of yours keep jabbing into every one of them."

"But it's the right thing to do."

"So is keeping your promises."

I pouted, crossing my arms the rest of the way.

Romero continued discussing my "training." I only half-listened. He gave me a row of bobby pins and told me how to use them. He discussed "proper technique" for holding my saber as well as my most loathsome topic: manipulation.

"Great, like how you manipulated me."

No response.

That shut him up. To him, my figure was my greatest weapon. I guess being puny as a sparrow was good for something.

Truth be told, I hated it. It made me feel disgusting. I wouldn't hear any more about it. Look what he had done to Hazel. I wouldn't be like him.

We followed the remnant crowd to the inn, toward the center of town. High above the village, a towering spire of rock cast a shadow over us. Beneath it stood a bouncing wooden building, The Canary Cage.

"This is the place," Romero said.

Of all the bars I had been in between Hazel's and mine, this was the classiest. A large baboon changeling played ragtime in the corner. I couldn't believe it—no broken glass, no tavern brawls, not even arm wrestling, which was almost a shame. It was a veritable paradise.

We sat at a table facing the bar. The staff were dressed in formal attire. The male waiters dressed in white dress shirts and bright red bow ties, and behind the bar was a lady.

Her skin appeared soft white, like a cloud, and she seemed innocent as a dove. She emerged in a crimson satin gown and pearls and tucked behind her back were two giant ivory eagle wings. They glowed a brighter silky white than her skin. She spoke like a sailor but looked like an angel. Her lemony-colored hair spun in long curls.

I say lemony because, while it was pleasant to look at, she was bitter about her appearance. But, I'm getting ahead of myself. She chewed out a few patrons for not paying their tabs and was the only ill-mannered person around.

Romero did all the talking. He told the waiter we wished to speak to a man named Jasper. The man nodded and walked off, tipping his hat to me as he went. Everyone here was super friendly.

When the waiter returned, they invited us over to the bar and told us it would be a while. He wasn't sure if it would be a little while or a long while, but rest assured, it would be "a while." *Fantastic.*

One by one, the patrons left. The ragtime pianist was replaced with a black panther changeling continuing the evening with candlelight jazz. The ladybird changeling began humming to herself.

"All right, what can I get you two?"

Her voice was sweet and twangy. Not gruff or coarse, but smooth, just rough enough to keep us on our toes, as if she brandished a whip with her speech. I had never heard an accent like hers before.

Before Romero could order, she grabbed my hand and gaped at my ring. "Oh my gosh! Congratulations to the happy couple. What a lovely gem. Want to see mine?" She flashed a marble-sized ring.

"Oh, we're not married," I began.

"Oh, so you're engaged. When's the wedding? I bet you'll look beautiful, but," she grabbed my shirt, inspecting it, "white's not your color."

"Oh well, we aren't . . . wait, really?"

"Oh, no, child. You could pull off a nice lavender or a cerulean for contrast."

What followed was a lengthy conversation between two women about fashion and clothes to which Romero rolled his eyes. As fewer customers drank, it was only us at the bar, give or take. Finally, he had enough.

"Yes, I'd love a drink," he interrupted.

"But I didn't offer you a drink."

"About thirty minutes ago you did. I'll take the hardest stuff you have and make it snappy."

The lady shook her head before grabbing a tray of empty glasses, heading off to the kitchen door.

"We'll talk later. I want to hear all about your weddin', puddin'."

As she walked away, I half laughed to myself. Out of the seat of her skirt was a white, feathery tail. I looked over to Romero, still a little nervous our lie would unravel.

"How was that?" I asked.

"Textbook. Let them believe what they want and the spell's cast," he said.

"I still don't feel right lying to people. But you could've been nicer to her, you know."

"And listen to you talk makeup next? Yeah, right. I need to be sober-minded. Just stick to the story and you'll be fine. Are you sure you don't have some demon in you?"

I frowned.

Remember what Shorty said at the bar fight? One of the most common and harshest slurs you could call a changeling was a demon. They called us evil, manipulative, deceiving, and cruel. I wanted none of it. Given my life, the title would suit me well, but it's not the person I wanted to be.

As the ladybird changeling got ready to return to the kitchen, the door swung open, nearly knocking over her row of glasses. A man with violet-colored skin approached from the other side of the door. Scales covered his face. Not only that, but his eyes were like mine, cat-eyed, only muddied. Horns rolled from both sides of his face like spirals of bone. He was just like me, tail and all.

The short changeling half stood on his toes to plant a wet one on her cheek. "And how's my favorite little pigeon pants?"

"Oh, stop. You'll make me drop my drinks. Not in front of the customers," she said, blushing.

She entered the kitchen, ruffling her wings.

"Stay beautiful, my treasure," he called back. "Now, are you the two who seek Jasper?"

Romero lifted his tired head up from his arm. "That would be us."

The man sauntered over to Romero with arms open wide. "Good to see you, Charles. How long has it been, huh? You look terrible. You could use a shave."

"Speak for yourself."

The man let loose a hearty laugh.

"And who is this?" He grabbed my hand with both of his. "What's your name, my dear?"

Never had I seen another pair of cat eyes.

"Sinopa."

Balls! Crap! Why did I say that?

I was too scared to look over at Romero.

The cat-eyed man kissed my hand. "Darling, the name's Jasper Rutledge. Charmed, I'm sure. Sinopa? Goblin, is it not?"

"Exactly. How did you know?"

"I've traveled the world and seen many a wonder. Goblin truly is a beautiful tongue. We had a young goblin sap here once. Poor thing. They ran the small thing out of the town gate. It was a shame. Here in Jarbah we seek the old way. We want everyone here to be welcome."

The lady changeling returned with a tankard of hard cider for Romero.

"Pidge, meet Sinopa and an old friend of mine."

"We've already met. Did you hear? They're engaged."

Jasper's jaw dropped. A wide, fanged grin took its place.

"The ol' sly fox finally bit the dust, did he? It's about time. How'd he manage that? Or better yet, Sinopa, how'd you hold him down? You pregnant? You're pregnant, aren't you?"

We all laughed, Romero a tad less than the rest.

"You best hold onto your peach, here, or you will have me cheating on my wife. This, my dear Sinopa, is one of my most prized possessions," he said, squeezing her shoulders.

Above him towered a row of heads mounted on the wall, heads of many animals: wolves, lions, rhinoceros, bears, lynx, tigers, the list goes on.

"I've hunted the world over, traded our prized ale across the entire globe, and have captured only the finest specimens. And this one was not in the mountains, jungles, or badland deserts but, of all places, the circus. She was the great Sonia Pidgeona Strignolli, the flying woman of wonder."

"I never chose that name," Sonia swore crossly.

Jasper pulled her neat white wings open. "Look at these beauties. Feel how soft they are. Such upper body strength like this you couldn't imagine."

Sonia flicked her ruffled wing shut with a gust of cold air.

"What's the matter, love?"

"We'll discuss it later," she shot coldly, returning to the kitchen.

"Guess I'm in trouble. Suppose when you get married it will be something to look forward to for you, too, am I right?"

A waiter came and whispered something in his ear. I heard the distinct words "pureblood" and "high wolf." Jasper blew him off with the bat of a hand.

"My apologies. Business never stops, am I right? Well, anyway, I found her and whisked her away from that dreadful place. What about you, Sinopa? I thought I knew all the changelings around these parts."

"I was hoping I could live here in Jarbah."

"A changeling returning home? Sounds like cause for celebration."

"I'm afraid we don't have the time," Romero butted in. "We were wondering what you knew about the imperials. Given your connections and knowledge of the area, that's why I came to you."

Jasper's smile widened. "Up to your old tricks again, ah? I like it. This guy, I love him. What's it this time? Sabotage? Blackmail? Larceny?"

Jasper had a habit of ending most sentences with a "yah" or an "ah." I suppose it was a regional dialect he'd picked up in his travels.

"Nothing big, just need to find someone."

"That much I can do, but I'm afraid the price has gone up."

"And here I thought we were partners."

"Yes, but business is business. You don't get to live like me working for free; plus, I have the entire Northstrand Navy at my back door."

"Forget it. The deal's off. Come on, Sinopa."

"Come, now, Charles, we'll discuss it over dinner. Let us feast. One of our own has come home. It's a rite of passage for all changelings."

"I'm afraid we must go."

"You can at least stay the night. Boys, show our honorable guest to his quarters—free of charge, of course."

Two men approached, following Romero upstairs. One had the head of a tiger and the other had grizzly gorilla biceps for arms. Both loomed over him, close by his side. I felt uneasy.

Sonia returned with a pint of coffee for Jasper. As she tried to reenter the kitchen, he pulled her wing. She winced, and he hugged her to his side.

"Sinopa, you simply must dine with us. It shall be a feast in your honor. Around here we call it the nesting ceremony. It's a tradition by which every changeling becomes a man or a woman. What do you say?"

I looked again to the dark stairs Romero had climbed. There wasn't a hint of him. I turned to Sonia who gave me a silent nod.

"What about R—I mean Charles?"

"Your fiancée is more than welcome to join us."

My stomach growled just then, so I agreed.

Jasper's fingers drummed on his cheek with a Cheshire grin. "Wonderful. Sonia, rally the cooks and prepare our fair Sinopa. Our sister has come home."

CHAPTER TWENTY-FOUR

My heart throbbed uneasily. I had failed in my one job—sticking to my story. Jasper didn't seem right, either. He was too kind, too sweet, and so happy. His "darlings" and "my sweets" were well-meaning at best, and creepy at worst.

Still, his kindness wasn't all bad. At the clap of his hands, two strong waiters hoisted my stool in the air and carted me upstairs to a room like a queen. My feet couldn't even touch the ground. Upon placing me down in the room, both kissed my hand and left me blushing. They left me in front of a vanity with my thoughts, wondering what the hell I had gotten myself into this time.

Moments later, Sonia entered.

"All right, puddin', let's get you fixed up," she said.

"Fixed?"

She opened a large walk-in closet with rows of gowns and dresses. Being a young farm girl, I had never seen so many dresses. I ran my hands up and down the variety of fabrics.

"See anything you like?"

I marveled at all the dresses in rainbow walls of fabric. At Sonia's suggestion, I picked a lavender gown. It was tight and slimming, with a row of lace above the knee. It even had a zipper for my tail. She had an uncanny eye for style. Sonia bestowed upon me a row of pearls and a tiara. I felt like a princess. I stared in the mirror enraptured. My thoughts kept turning to Cheryl, Romero, and then home.

"What's wrong?"

"Nothing. I'm fine. It's beautiful, but it's not me."

"I think you look lovely."

"Is Charles going to be okay?"

Sonia sighed and began twiddling with her pearls. "Having second thoughts about marriage?"

I nodded. "You could say something like that. The way Jasper spoke about him didn't exactly set my mind at ease."

Dare I say it, I worried for the crook. I massaged my ring. There was no telling how much I could tell Sonia, though.

She began tying my hair up in a bun. I noticed in the mirror, when she turned to fetch some pearl earrings, faint purple bruising beneath her wings and shoulder blades.

"Well, maybe it's best. You should fully know him before you go through with it."

"Did you?"

There was a pause.

"You've nothing to worry about with Jasper. I know him. He won't hurt you. Nor Charles."

I felt more relieved to hear that.

We dressed to kill. Little did I know what would become of us.

Sonia led the way and kept telling me to "smile, this is a feast."

We grew mutual respect in our shared disdain for the men in our lives. Even though our relationship stood founded on lies, she would become my best friend and greatest enemy.

Downstairs, food covered a long oak table end-to-end. A large roast, carrots, potatoes, fruits, yes, even plums, and desserts as far as the eye could see. Jasper sat at the head, and he ushered his wife to sit beside him. I sat as the maiden of honor across the table at the other end. Three waiters stood waiting to pull out my chair and prepare my plate. I insisted that I could do it myself, but they ignored me.

"So nice of you to join us, Sinopa. Eat, my dear. Welcome home."

The food was delicious. There wasn't a single dish, not a single bite, without perfection.

"Boys, fetch her fiancée if you would be so kind."

Three men went up the stairs, and one pulled up a chair to my right.

"So, lost sister of ours, tell us about yourself."

I shoved another spoonful into my mouth. I hadn't thought this far ahead.

Think, Sinopa. Think.

"Wouldn't you rather tell me about yourself first? You're the host. I'd like to know more about how you two met."

Sonia pulled at the pearls around her collar.

"Strange, but it is your party. Ah, yes, how we met. Young love is a beautiful thing. Yes, I, much like your future husband, was a journeyman of sorts."

Jasper made a grand gesture to the walls. Heads of exotic animals of all sizes mounted both sides. Swords, artist portraits, and marble statues proclaimed his glory.

"We sought gold, riches, fame, and women. But all of that changed when we stumbled across something new. You see, there are ruins in these lands. Ruins of civilization before the rise of myst and the fall of machina. Naturally, the brave—"

"More like reckless," his wife butted in.

"Yes, reckless men—we scavenged it for treasure. What I unearthed you couldn't possibly fathom. There were records, legends of a nation. A nation of prosperity where changelings could walk free, live, and even reign among man, or the "humes" as they called them. It has now become my life's work to bring this dream to fruition . . . along with crafting the most excellent liquor. I mean, what's an empire without booze, am I right?"

Another spoonful of potatoes crammed into my cheeks. I had to think of something fast. The three men returned from upstairs. My eyes searched. Immediately, I noticed Romero was missing. Their words confirmed it: Romero had left with the message that I should meet him at the cornerstone arch when I was ready.

"Such a pity. He'll miss all the festivities. Now, sister dear, where did you say you were from?"

I chewed slowly and swallowed. There was an expectant silence. My eyes shifted on Sonia, then Jasper, and back to her.

"Darling, you didn't answer her question," said Sonia.

Jasper dropped his fork. It clanked on his steak knife.

"What was that, Pidge?"

Two men began circling to the back of her chair.

"I said—"

The two changelings stared down at her. She grabbed Jasper's hand and put on a weak smile.

"I said you didn't answer her question, love. Don't you want to tell her how we met, puddin'?"

He patted her hand. "Yes, yes, of course."

The two men stepped back to the wall, watching and waiting.

He continued, "Yes, who could forget that tale? Who could forget how I rescued you?"

Sonia's eyes darted to the floor.

"After I had parted ways with Charles, I headed to the hill country of Geneva Paradiso. Who could forget how I whisked away the fair maiden from the bonds of the big top? We released them all, didn't we, dear?"

Sonia refused to look up from the floor.

"Don't be shy in front of our company, dear."

A thud bounced the table from underneath.

She nodded.

"You see, Sinopa, my wonderful wife wasn't always so wonderful."

"Stop, please," she begged.

"Now, love, I'm just answering her question as you told me. What's a good husband who doesn't listen to his wife, eh?

"The circus was an awful place. Humes would gather from all the villages bringing their snot-nosed brats to see the 'beasts' in cages. And the circus knew what to do to those who misbehaved. Poor, poor, little Sonia,"

"Please stop."

"All she wanted was a better view of the animals and the show. But when they found out she could do it for free, that simply wouldn't do. So, they incarcerated her. Charges were theft and practicing magic. That's another thing they brand on us young, Sinopa. Those filthy humes. Those disgusting sorcerers give us changelings a bad name. Not all of us can mold the myst to our will."

I took a sip of my drink and nodded. I held my tail up with one hand to keep it from sagging. My poker face needed help. I couldn't show that they scared me.

The door opened to the banquet hall. A tall figure walked in. His face was that of a tiger, not a man, only stone white instead of the usual orange. Leather armor, stained red, covered his shirt. Noticeably missing was his long feline tail. The only shimmer of humanity in the man not covered in fur was his left hand hidden in a black glove.

"Ah, good evening, Mr. Cutswell. So glad you could join us. We're in the middle of a nesting celebration. It's turned sour at the moment."

The big cat man stared him down, silently scanning the room.

"What's the matter, Puss-puss? Have you any mice?"

Cutswell growled and reached for his hand axes at his side. The servants rushed to meet him.

"I'm only kidding," said Jasper. "Come, now, come. Please sit. You must pardon his manners, Sinopa. Desmodius is a rather ill-fated bounty hunter of these parts. He hasn't caught a man in months. He's a man of few words. The cat has always got his tongue, get it? Get it? Ah, you'll get it later. In these past few years, we've become more like brothers. Haven't we, Dezzy?"

He grunted, rolling his eyes and sitting down at the table.

"Now, where were we? Oh, yes—"

"Please stop! That's enough!" Sonia screamed.

She pushed herself back and stood up, flaring her wings at the table. Two men behind her grabbed her shoulders and the wing stems.

"Perhaps you best head to bed, dearest. You appear to have had too much to drink. Don't worry, dear, I'll join you after the festivities are over."

Her wings slumped to her back, and her head hung low. The two men began escorting her from behind toward the stairs.

"No, wait!" I interrupted. "It's fine. She can stay."

"I beg your pardon?" Jasper said.

Sonia looked at me, shaking her head. Her entire body shook.

"I'm the maid of honor, right? I'd like her to stay."

Footsteps approached the back of my chair. Jasper shook his head at them.

"Rightfully said, dear sister. If you wish it, she can stay."

The men removed their hands from behind Sonia and took a place at the table with the rest of us. I looked over at her and she mouthed a "thank you."

I nodded.

Jasper raised a glass for a toast. "Come, now, let's drop all this talk of the past. Let bygones be bygones. This is a party. Let us eat, drink, and be merry, for tomorrow we die."

𝄢

THE PARTY WENT on late into the night. Jasper didn't seem too bad after that. It could have been the booze, though. Angela never let me drink much if she could help it. So, to me, the riotous and rebellious girl I was, the wine tasted like honey and flowed like water.

Music played, and we danced. It was nice to be the belle of the ball, all the boys wanting to dance with me. I felt special. All eyes were on me —and with longing, not disdain, scorn, hatred, or disgust. My feet danced on clouds, and one by one, the boys would cut in. Well, most danced with the kitchen staff, but it was more attention than I had received in years. Everyone seemed to have a good time. All save one.

In the corner, Mr. Cutswell sat nursing a tankard of ale. He slumped over with his hand to his head, avoiding eye contact. I excused myself and approached. I don't know why I felt bad for him. Perhaps because he'd been mocked in front of random strangers and had not gotten what he'd been pursuing for so long. I blamed the booze.

As I approached, he was taking another sip of his drink.

"Excuse me, Mr. Cats—I mean Cutswell?"

The tiger's head turned up at me. His eyes bulged and glared. His throat growled and droplets of alcohol dripped from his whiskers.

"Yes, sorry to bother you. I was just wondering if maybe you would like to dance. I saw you sitting here alone and just thought . . ."

His claws retracted, clicking against his thumb. He shook his head.

"Sorry. I just thought no one ought to be alone." I walked away and the nearest waiter joined me in a dance. Desmodius looked up from his drink a few times but always returned to it. I danced for a good thirty minutes before I felt a tap on my shoulder.

My dance partner took a few steps back. I turned around and it was Desmodius. He jerked his head for my partner to beat it. The circle around either stepped back or stopped dancing altogether. The music died. He shot the violinist a death glare and nodded for him to play. The violinist tugged at his collar, and the band began a tango.

The big cat did a circle around me, his eyes fixed on mine. His unblinking pupils glowed unnaturally, blue cat eyes like mine. He held out his hand for me. I took hold and we were off.

Quick, quick, slow, slow. I had to admit Old Whiskers was light on his feet. To me, he moved too close and too fast. My feet fell behind and stumbled until, to my surprise, he lifted them off the floor and placed them back at the downbeat. He nodded at me. I could keep pace once more.

Take notes, boys. Such gentle ferocity in a man is electrifying. His shoulders were tough yet plushily pelted. His hands were gentle yet prickly clawed. His grip was tender—yet rough. It gives me goosebumps just thinking about it. Oh, to be young again . . .

He twirled me and continued to dance with my back to his front. His whiskers brushed through my hair. He wasn't tall. As the music came to a close, he went for a twirl, then a dip. My world appeared upside down, and the surrounding crowd clapped and cheered. He let me up, and I gave a bow.

We danced together for the rest of the night. No one dared butt in on Cutswell. Soon most of the men disappeared. Half the band left, and the cooks went with them. Old Whiskers had a groove. Smooth tunes glided across the banquet hall. His hands wrapped around my waist. My arms rested on his shoulders, cradling his neck.

Jasper called out from across the room, cackling to him, "Take it easy on her, Dezzy. She just became a woman this afternoon and is engaged for some time soon. I don't want to hear about her fiancé placing a bounty on the bounty hunter, ah?"

Cutswell shot him a glare, and he left for the other room. We were alone. It was just me, the big cat, and a lone clarinetist. The whole night he hadn't spoken a single word.

I tried to break the silence.

"I must say, I'm pleasantly surprised. You have the magic touch."

Cutswell remained silent, only acknowledging my praise with nods and remaining distant. His eyes remained straight ahead, staring off into space. Even then he seemed searching.

What was he thinking? What was he hiding? And why didn't he speak?

I noticed his eye, his left eye, had a long gash above and below. It appeared fresh, as damp crimson dabbed the surrounding fur.

I reached my hand toward his cut and, immediately, as without thought, he batted it away with cat-like reflexes.

"I was just looking. Geez. Sensitive, aren't we? Are you at least okay?"

He nodded.

"Good. I can't help but feel this conversation is one-sided. Aren't you happy you danced? Can you at least tell me that?"

"Yes," he replied.

His voice bellowed strong and resounding. It was like he spoke into a barrel.

"So you can talk?" I laughed.

He nodded.

"Well, good, I'm glad you're happy."

"Overjoyed."

"Excellent. As I said, you're an amazing dancer. I've had a wonderful time."

His hands gently pulled mine away from his neck to my sides.

"How'd you learn to dance like that?" I asked.

He remained silent.

"Cat got your tongue?"

"When you are out chasing your mark, you have got to put your passion into it. You need to stalk your prey. Be on the prowl and pounce on the prey before you. You can't stop until you find what you are looking for."

I walked my fingers up to his chin. "And what is it you are looking for?"

He snatched my hand again and tossed it aside. "I have to leave." He walked over and began to put on his coat by the door. You could tell from behind he was indeed a tailless tiger.

"Oh, come on, you can tell me."

"My honor—I find me a mark, I restore my place in the pack."

"Well, Mr. Cutswell, I hope you find whatever it is you're looking for."

He nodded, expressing his thanks and kissing my hand. "Call me Des."

As he turned to leave, I asked him to stay, suggesting we "merengue" someplace suitable. Keep in mind, I was slightly tipsy. Okay, very tipsy.

The big cat shook his head and walked out the door without looking back. And so, the game of cat and mouse had begun.

CHAPTER TWENTY-FIVE

S onia was cleaning up at the bar outside the banquet hall. "So, how'd it go?" she asked.

"Wonderful. I've never felt this . . . special."

She grinned, wiping down the bar. "I've never seen Desmodius do anything but growl and sulk. How'd you manage that?"

I shrugged. "A woman's touch, I guess."

"Yeah, well, your woman's touch really did a number on everyone else. The rest of the men were out here drowning their sorrows because of how they had struck out again."

"Sorry."

"Are you kidding? We made a killing. Jasper's not stupid. That's why he built the nesting banquet hall beside the bar. No need to apologize."

"So they really all left, didn't they?" I asked.

Sonia nodded. The bar indeed was empty. Not a soul dared speak.

"Well, that's not an excuse for us gals not to drink through the night." She shook her head. "I think you've had enough."

"Hey, I'm only a little tipsy." I released a very unladylike belch.

"Okay, perhaps I'm a little drunk, but momma knows how to hold her liquor."

That was a bold-faced lie.

"And still," I continued, "that's nothing a little hair of the dog that bit me can't fix."

"I'll see what I can do," Sonia said, returning to the kitchen.

I sat at the bar and looked over the trophy heads. All of them stared glassy-eyed and gasping for air. I entered a staring contest with a boar. His eyes had a thousand-yard stare, and his dark throat seemed screaming endlessly.

"What are you looking at?" I drunkenly asked, throwing him the double guns.

My head slammed on the table. I could have slept there with no regrets. Sonia prodded me awake with a glass in her hand. In my blurred vision, she was a blond angel over me.

"Thanks, Angie," I told her, and threw it down the hatch.

The brine was vinegary and lemony. Earthy dirt aftertaste rose in my throat. I gagged in a coughing fit.

"What was that?"

"An old herbal remedy. A pinch of ginseng root, nutmeg, beet juice, lemon juice, apple cider vinegar, a hint of ginger, plenty of water, and a blue lotus bloom—otherwise known as the Jerbalian moon juice. It'll help with your hangover."

"But I don't have a hang—"

Instantaneously, a throbbing pain shot to my forehead.

"There it is," Sonia giggled. "It speeds up your heart rate and metabolism. There's more in the back if you like."

My stomach somersaulted from the vinegar brine. I lay over the bar, holding it. Sonia passed me a bucket just in case.

"First time?" she asked.

I nodded with a groan.

A rumble rose from the deepest pit of my stomach. My head swayed over the bucket in my lap. Sonia raced around the counter and held my hair back. I felt as though I was emptying my entire self into the bucket. She rubbed my back. I swore I would never drink again each time I came up for air.

"Never again." I spewed.

"That's what they all say," replied Sonia.

When I finished, she took her towel and wiped the corners of my cheeks. I began to feel better, much better.

She poured me another glass of the seltzer-like brew. It was hard not to spit it straight back out. Sonia drank hers like a champ, but then again, she can be sour herself sometimes.

My head cleared, but my balance was still off. My mind focused, the fog cleared, and my heart raced. A little known fact about ginseng is that it speeds up your heart rate. I begged her for something sweet to kill the taste. Anything, even a sip of wine. Heck, even beer. I was more than willing to vomit again to mask the terrible flavor.

"Afraid we're fresh out. Jasper disappeared in the cellar some time ago to change the kegs."

"Well, what's taking him so long? Let me change it." I staggered over behind the bar to the trap door of the cellar.

"What would you know about changing a keg?" Sonia asked.

"Come on, I've run a bar before. I think I know how to change a keg." I pulled open the hatch and a cold breeze blew through my hair.

Sonia grabbed my arm. "Don't go down there."

"And why not?" I protested.

She pulled at her pearls, tight around her collar. Her eyes focused on the trophies over the bar. "You're still tipsy. You could get hurt."

"It's just a keg. I'll be fine."

She grabbed my arm again. Her eyes nervously blinked. "Just be careful."

I climbed down the ladder, losing my footing on the damp bars once or twice. I could see Sonia staring down into the darkness above me. Had I been entirely sober, I would have hyped up the scene to scare her.

My wobbly legs staggered in the dark, supporting myself on the wet brickwork. Down the hall, torches flickered. Not much windmill power underground, I supposed. I followed the narrow passageway and reached a torch, and a fork in the path. Across from me were rows and rows of hefty wooden casks piled to the ceiling.

To my left, a row of stairs stood from which I imagined they received their stock. I grabbed the torch and approached the large room. On my way, a frigid breeze blew through my thin dress. I shivered.

Why would there be a breeze underground?

I turned to my right. There was a black curtain drifting back and forth on the wall. I pulled at it. Behind it was another long, dark corridor. I looked at the room with the casks and back to the corridor and shrugged. It was none of my business to be snooping around down there. I hooked up the keg lines for the beer I liked. Not that hard.

Where is Jasper?

They branded all the kegs and casks with a picture of his fanged smile.

As I passed the curtain and heard a groan echoing from the other side.

"Jasper?"

I entered behind the curtain. It had been a while since either Sonia or I had seen him. Somebody had to make sure he was all right, even if he was a bit of a creep. A faint shimmer glowed at the end.

I called out again, "Jasper? This is not funny."

As I walked further, the brick walls turned to rows of steel bars. Cells rowed the halls. I peered inside one. A male wolf changeling lay shackled to the floor. A guard uniform was slashed to rags in the corner. In the next, a lady lynx lay in a horrifying position on the wall. In another, a boar-like humanoid was impaled on a spike. Rats swarmed around the rotting corpse.

And it only got worse. The next cells held humans, humans treated like animals. Muzzles, undersized cages, and food bowls lay tossed about. The stagnant air hung thick with the stench of feces. Along the walk, small grates trickled myst rising from the ground, creating a faint current at my bare ankles. My heels knocked on the stone, echoing in the chamber. Faint sobs echoed as I approached the cells in the dark.

I reached the light at the end of the hall. Two torches stood beside an iron door with a small hatch. I had to find Jasper and get out of here. I had to get help or the police.

Can I even go to the police?

A continual dread reverberated in my head. The thought kept hounding me, "You shouldn't be here." Over and over it was, "You shouldn't be here. You shouldn't be here."

The metal screeched as I pulled the hatch to see what was inside.

In the dimly lit room, a man sat on his knees chained to the floor by his ankles. They had cut his white shirt open. Long red lacerations severed sections of his chest in crossed cuts. A long, button jacket sat on his shoulders. Purple knots bruised a scruffy chin.

It was Romero.

I yanked open the iron door. It clanged against the brick wall. I dropped to my knees beside him.

"Romero? Romero, what happened?"

His eyes glazed white. Manacles cuffed his arms behind his back. I tugged at the shackles on his ankles. It was no use. They wouldn't budge.

I thumbed through my hair looking for a hairpin. It was time to put my training to the test. I fiddled with the locks, all the while offering him encouraging words. I kept asking him questions and begged him to stay awake.

The cheap metal hairpins kept breaking. It was a good thing I had plenty. I only undid one lock. By the time I figured it out, I went through ten hairpins.

Down the hall, footsteps approached. Hard thuds bellowed on the stone floor. I lightly slapped Romero awake across his face.

"Stay with me. I'm going to get you out of this."

His eyes blinked and shuttered. The footsteps came closer. I had to work fast. My fingers fiddled with the lock behind his back. I wasn't sure if it was the ginseng or the pressure, but my heart pulsated through my skin.

TING. I looked down at the lock. The pin snapped.

The iron door slammed shut. I was too late.

A ruthless, toothy smile gleamed through the hatch. A midnight, fanged figure loomed down as a spectacular head through the window.

"Tsk, tsk, tsk, sister dear. You have a habit for trouble, don't you, now?"

"Jasper let me out. We've got to help him."

"No, I believe he's staying, I'm afraid."

His accent dropped.

"Jasper? Why? These people . . . what happened to equality?"

"Yes, but equality starts with us first. The changeling race must have retribution. All wrongs must be made right."

My head throbbed in my hangover. I heard his words, but they made little sense.

"Understand, sister, I loathe this work as much as you do. But I must prune the limbs that bear the fruit of the future. And if they resist pruning, dismemberment. You must understand. The ends will justify the means. The High Wolf must ascend; the purebloods must be restored to the clergy."

I shook my head in disbelief at what I was hearing.

"What do you know of the purebloods?"

His smile grew wider. "They're the clergy of the past, and the protectors of machina and the evils of the old age. Praise be to the High Wolf that I should be so blessed to be of pureblood myself, as is Cutswell."

I latched onto Romero, my fingers unavoidably getting caught in some of his wounds.

Who knew Jasper was a pureblood, too?

"But, sadly, I was unfit for service. I couldn't open the throne room of the War Pig. The vestige was not mine, and I was not worthy of rule. He's sent Desmodius and me to track down the true called one: you."

A poster flew through the slot of the door and fell at my knees. It was his face, not mine.

"I avenged you on the night of your arrival personally. Behind the scenes, my wolves held off most of the cultists' onslaught of the library so you'd make your escape. I made sure there was enough crime to bring the master to your cell to save you. The sorceress who hurt you—me! All me! I framed you and sowed all the seeds leading here."

My head pounded. "No, this can't be right."

"You're the key to absolute power, the vestige! That filthy feline Cutswell shall rue his birth. If he only knew who he had danced with. Now I shall steal his crown in the Archaeopteryx. Join me, dear sister. I can take you to meet the great wolf father. The empire shall—"

"I'll never join you."

Jasper sighed, shaking his head. "Pity it has to be this way. You really were quite the catch."

"Let us go now."

"And why would I do that?" He laughed. "'Let us go now.' Whine, whine, whine. You really are cute. Yes, old Charles here will fetch a hefty sum from the imperials. The bounty on his head is a mile high. Guess you should have taken the bargain, then, ah?"

Romero's chest skin peeled like an onion. His body swayed back and forth.

Jasper continued, "Yes, at least Dezzy will catch something after all, come morning."

I turned to Romero's mangled flesh and back to Jasper. "If I join you, will you let him go?"

Jasper's clawed fingers drummed on his chin.

"Perhaps."

The iron door opened and he stepped aside. I stood and walked toward him to the exit. He slammed the door and grabbed my wrist. His claws sank into my skin.

"But only on one condition."

His eyes stared down at me in my dress. He began to laugh as he pulled me past the dark curtain.

CHAPTER TWENTY-SIX

He'd done it. I don't know how, but he did. I thought I could escape that life, yet somehow, against everything I believed, he forced me back.

I experienced all the sensations again. My legs swayed. His needle crumpled my balance with its familiar sting. My eyes widened. My heart raced.

This is for Romero. I must save him and prove my innocence. I must stop Jasper.

I will not glorify that monster in this. Heaven knows he wanted more sickos like him, so I'll skip to the aftermath.

As you can imagine, this is difficult for me to discuss. I will not glorify him in this. It's what he would want.

He forced me to relive every painful memory from my youth in a single evening. The lightheadedness blanketed over my mind. I lived in beats of my past. The needle entered my blood. Every feeling heightened. A cold knife pierced my skin. A sweaty sock gagged between my teeth. My eyes stung, crying helpless tears at the mirrored ceiling, so I could relive the past twice over. So much blood. So, so much blood.

I needed out. I begged to escape and called for anyone to help. My brain went over every name I knew, but no one came. All my cries muffled through the night. I was alone.

Trust no one. You'll always end up on your back begging for mercy.

Jasper chuckled, suggesting another round. He stood up and began rummaging through a dresser drawer and pouring a glass of wine.

I sobbed, shaking my head. My eyes stared up at my mangled body and bawled. My scars were on full display.

Thin twine bound my wrists. They chaffed on the two posts above me. My purse dangled from one.

I have to fight back. I will fight if it kills me. At least I won't die a victim. No, not any longer.

My limbs tingled without feeling in my nerves. My fingers picked the jingling zipper. His back remained to me. He pulled a long syringe from under a pair of socks. My body cringed. My toes curled.

The purse growled slowly open. Minnie's book took up most of the space. I caught something round and cold, the lipstick. It was time to knock him dead or die trying.

Jasper shot around, wrenched my purse from me, and threw it on the floor.

"What have we here?"

My fingers uncurled and he held the lipstick in his hands. He snickered with a twisted grin.

"I knew you would come around. Allow me."

I choked, trying to laugh.

That's right. Take the bait.

As he pulled the cap, his body froze mid-expression. He collapsed, paralyzed. The vial syringe shattered beneath him on the floor. His eyes searched and a small trickle of blood descended his wrist. Minnie was right: I felt better.

I pulled with all my might to be free. The bonds snapped. Joy washed over me. I was free. I couldn't believe it. Free.

It took all my strength to stand up. I gathered my belongings. This time he was frozen on the floor—to watch. I spit in his face. My heel attempted to stamp, but I nearly fell over. He'd get what was coming to him later. I hobbled as fast as I could.

I'd come a long way. I was no longer the frightened little girl I once was. My monsters would never win, not if I could help it. Jasper was going down.

I swayed bowlegged down the cellar stairs. My legs waddled in opposite directions. My sides hurt. Red hand-shaped welts lined my throat. My once-neat auburn hair lay frizzled and in rats. Trudging down to the cellar and trying not to stumble, I couldn't help but remember my youth. This hadn't been the first time I felt sore, violated, and messy. I just hoped it would be the last. My mind wandered back to that fateful night when I left Pop-pop.

❧

A BUCKET of water was thrown in my face.

"Oi, get up."

I coughed as a goblin man stood on a stool over me. Another, younger goblin cowered behind the stool. My eyes searched for any sign of Havish since the incident. It'd been only a few hours.

"It's movin', Herb. It's moving."

My hair stuck to my face, and my torn footsie pajamas stuck to my legs.

"Shut up, you. I know it's moving. What? You don't think I see it's moving?"

I cowered on the floor. Two green faces towered over me in a strange place.

"Where's Pop-pop?" I asked.

The goblin on the stool laughed, lighting a fat cigar.

"I was the highest bidder. From now on I'm your daddy now. This is Aldephos," he said, pointing to the goblin cowering behind the stool.

"Get up from behind there. I'll show you how we break them in," Daddy barked.

Aldephos got up from behind the stool. They brought me into another room. My favorite pajamas were stripped and tossed into the furnace before my very eyes. I stood up tall and Daddy took measurements with a piece of twine, tying knots at certain lengths.

"You need to know all your girls' measurements and price them accordingly," Daddy said to Aldephos—I knew him better as Al. Daddy's full name was Herb Pater. We never called him it if we were smart. Now I'd never call him "Daddy."

He gave me fresh clothes comprised of cheetah and hyena pelts. Feathers lined the low-cut collar. I had never had clothes that fit before. I missed Pop-pop too much to enjoy the new clothes.

Tears welled up in my eyes. I cried and begged to see Pop-pop. I wouldn't listen to a single thing Pater said and threw a fit.

Immediately, he grabbed a poker and instructed Aldephos to watch. My back was cracked bloody, and he cracked Al next for looking away. Pater dragged me upstairs and I fell on a bed. I was told to think about what I had done. The wind blowing through the open window stung the cuts.

An hour later, Al drew me a cold bath upstairs. The cold water soothed my back and bruises. I drew him close at the brim of the tiny tub and hugged him. His kindness would be the only thing that would keep me going. I didn't know at the time that it was planned.

Pater would use this scheme many a time. Only, he'd do the same thing. He would clean my cuts, apologize, and tell me I was pretty.

That was how they worked. They manipulated me in how they beat me and berated me to be and fit a certain way. Then they fixed me—and I loved them. But why did I love them? I don't know.

It's like, after everything they did to me, the single moment they performed an act of love, it covered a multitude of sins. They broke me, they fixed me, and then they owned me. But I didn't know it at the time. If I recall, he even mocked me that the only way anyone would ever love me was on my back.

Pater was a disgrace to the goblin race. People think goblins are savage and stupid and evil, but all these are broad over-generalizations. Goblins are proud, noble people. They live off the land and by their means. Not a single resource is wasted. Our land dwindled more and more, and humans encroached more on our home. My people—yes, even though they are not of my blood, they are still my people—have been pushed to the brink of extinction by fallacies.

Goblins and man are equal. Changelings and man are equal. Just as man and woman are equal. Are we different in physicality and nature? Yes. But in terms of worth of dignity and respect—yes, we are equal. We are only different in the roles and purposes given to us on God's green earth. Rejection of this by no means nullifies it. I only say this because I want people to realize we are defined by our actions, not by our parents.

Pater exploited a loophole and requirement in goblin law for profit. There is a law that man must not be alone, and they are a lesser man for it. In goblin society, man is only a man upon marriage or consummate act thereof. Hence, the house was named the *bildungsroman*. It became a detestable place to Big Chief and Havish. They advocated for its destruction for years. If you ask me, a man's not a man until they know how to treat a lady. But, hey, what do I know? I'm just a looney old bird dwelling in the past.

I only made things worse for them. Pater advertised me as an odd attraction for the place and rounded up heaps of cash. I'd rather not go too deep into the details for obvious reasons, of course. I've got to protect the kiddies and pups in the room, and more importantly, my words can't do those women the justice they deserve.

I just feel you've stuck with me this long, you have the right to know. One day, I know all wrongs will be made right. Not by Jasper's warped hands, or even my own.

Back then, Havish visited me when he could. Of course, when Pater found out, he would spike the price. Soon Pop-pop couldn't afford to visit much, but he was willing to pay any price to see me.

The other girls and I didn't get along very well. Aldephos was the one I saw the most. He'd sneak me blackberries in the springtime, as he knew they were my favorite. He read me bedtime stories in place of Havish. I'd get beaten for it, and so would he. Pater expected him to carry on the business. When he'd beat him, his fixing was always, "You're my brother, and I love you. So I have to be tough on you."

To be honest, Al was more my brother than his. Funny—looking back now, it doesn't hurt anymore. It will always haunt me and has been an inescapable hurdle in my thinking. Their game owns me. I'm a double slave.

Now, the phantom pain lingers, but the wound is sealed. It's a scar, not a scab. It tells a story. Let's not pick at it anymore.

CHAPTER TWENTY-SEVEN

I undid Romero's cuffs with the keys I'd stolen from Jasper and helped him to his feet. My plan was set into motion. We needed to escape by daybreak. Who knew how long that lipstick would last?

Romero's cuffs clinked to the floor. We had to move fast. He leaned and I had to drag his legs along, because he could barely walk. It didn't help that I'm such a short little freak.

As I passed the curtain, I had to set him down against the wall. Gosh, he was heavy. I slapped him several times on both cheeks, trying to force him to get a grip.

"Romero look at me. Romero, work with me, dear."

He turned his head and blinked. I steadied him between my two hands.

"I'm going to get us out of here, okay? But you've got to work with me. I'm too weak to carry you up these steps or up that ladder. So you are going to have to help me, all right?"

He remained unresponsive. There were only two ways out as far as I knew: the stairs, which lead to staff quarters and the loading dock, and the ladder underneath the bar. The stairs would be much easier, but it would be asking for capture. I would be under the same treatment as

Romero if they caught me. The thought of having my chest filleted like that gave me chills.

I climbed the ladder to see if anyone was around. I had no idea if I could get Romero out this way, but it was my only hope. The damp metal rungs slipped in my fingers. My tipsiness had settled, but the ladder was by no means an easy climb. I pushed open the trap door. The door creaked and came down with a thud. So much for stealth.

I poked my head out like an anxious gopher over the bar.

Sitting across at one table, Sonia turned my way, sipping a Jerbalian moon juice. "Sinopa?"

My head popped down behind the counter. I heard her heels approach.

I'm a goner. Crap. Crap. Crap!

She came around the counter to see me squatting. "What are you doing?"

"Nothing," I lied.

I'm such a terrible liar.

Sonia pulled me to my feet.

"Well, sit down. I'll get you that wine. You've disappeared for, like, forever."

"I'm . . . I . . ."

She rushed off into the kitchen. I shut the trapdoor and paced the front of the bar.

Could I really trust her? Everyone has turned on me so far.

She came back and set a small shot on the counter. Maybe she was just as clueless as I was. *She's his wife. She has to know.*

"Sonia, I need your help."

"I reckon so. You were down there for, like, an hour and still hooked up the lines wrong."

"It's Jasper."

Sonia's demeanor changed.

"He's crazy," I continued. "There are people trapped down there, and Romero—well, Charles—I need your help to get out of here."

"You went snooping around, didn't you?"

I nodded.

"I'm sorry. There's nothing I can do."

"But Sonia, they had my friend chained up in the basement. He can't even walk upright. I need your help. Come morning, there is no help for him."

"You know what Jasper would do to me if he found out I helped you?"

She turned around to reveal the bruises on the back of her neck.

"It's okay. We can get help. I'll bring the police. We can escape and I can get you out of here. Don't you want to leave?"

"Don't you think I've tried? We've all tried."

"We? Who's 'we?'"

Sonia let out a long sigh. Her eyes never raised from the floor. She walked to the far end of the bar. She stretched out her hand, stroking the head of a lynx.

"Meet Lady Gloria Lynxatious Tesla, famed Aristocrat on vacation in the keys. Jasper begged her to join the cause of the new order. She held some influence and could 'donate her progeny' to the empire's ranks. When she refused . . ." The head fell off the wall.

She continued, "Or perhaps you'd like to meet Chief Maximus Jumbo Dublunski of the Aerogapolian police force. Poor, poor Jumbo. I liked Jumbo. He had a beautiful wife. She tried to help me, too. But the Chief refused to look the other way, so she died first. Murdered before our very eyes. We were all forced to watch. I can still hear his—"

Her voice broke.

"Then, after he still wouldn't give in, they killed him, too. His final scream is immortalized here."

Tears hit the floor. She couldn't look the trophies in the eye.

"Look around you, Sinopa. These are his trophies. All the reminders of the times I've tried and failed. He placed them hanging over me as reminders of why I can never leave. Because when I try," she wiped her tears away, "people die."

I stared at the rows of trophies on the wall. They were no longer just heads now—they were faces. Men, women, sons, and daughters all crying out for mercy. Tears welled up in my eyes. They stared into the heavens with heads cocked back and eyes unblinking, appearing enlightened in their agony. They understood the evil of man.

"I'm so sorry, Sonia. I really am, but it doesn't have to be this way. You can—"

"I don't want you to die, too."

"Fine, then not for me. But for Charles. He's lying down there and he'll die, come morning, if he stays here. If we get caught, he dies. If we stay, he dies."

"And you could, too."

I paused.

"That's a chance I'm willing to take. He's my friend, and I'd rather die than see him suffer. Don't you think he deserves that chance? You could fly away from here."

"Oh, hardy har har. 'Sonia's a bird. Don't you feel free with those wings of yours? You can fly,'" she mocked. "All my life these wings of mine have been my biggest cage. My feathers are my greatest fetters. I'm a freak."

"Okay, maybe that was the wrong thing to say," I said.

It *really* was the wrong thing to say.

"The point is, if you stop, if you give up now, everything they gave up would have been for nothing. Everything they went through. Everything they endured. It would have been for nothing."

Sonia curled her hair and looked at the smooth elephant face of Jumbo the police chief. Her wings unfurled in a gust of wind. They glistened in the dim light underneath. Her body stood as a glowing cross.

"Where is he?"

"By the curtain, against the wall."

She slammed open the trap door.

"I hope you're right about this." She dove. A whooshing sound resounded in the darkness.

Beneath me, there was the beating of wings. It was rhythmic and heavy. They were her war drums bellowing in the dark. Her wings pounded faster and faster. The drumming came closer and closer until, suddenly, Sonia burst from the hole in the floor as a billowing cyclone. She hovered over the hole holding Romero in her arms.

Heads came crashing to the ground from the rush of wind. She hovered. Her head grazed the ceiling, allowing every face, every gruesome failure, and every shortcoming, every last one to fall. They would no longer have a hold over her. She pulled Romero up once more, closer to her body. Her arms grew tired. She gave me one last glance before coming down and resting him over the bar.

The walls stood bare. Not a single semblance of death hung over her. Sonia was free, too. I threw my arms around her and hugged her over the bar.

"You better get going. It's almost morning."

I grabbed Romero and threw his arm over my shoulder. "Are you going to be okay?"

"I'll be fine. I'm his wife, remember? I think I know how to handle him. Now get going. If he finds out you're gone, he may come looking."

"I'll come back for you. I promise."

"Beat it! Now!"

I pulled Romero close to me and ran as fast as my legs could take me.

WE RAN—WELL, I carried Romero along—as fast as I could. There was no rhyme or reason as to where I was going. I just knew I had to get away and fast. There was no way my head would be next. My thoughts turned to the police, but then to Jumbo. They probably wouldn't listen. They could even work for Jasper as far as I knew. I already knew Cobarde worked for the wyrm.

Romero seemed much more alert now. His eyes were open and looking about. I pushed branches aside and began stumbling through the jungle. Frogs and locusts hissed under the shadowy canopy. The occasional bat and bird whistled or peeped.

Twigs snapped beneath our feet, low branches cracked back in our faces. I lost one of my heels in a small brook and tripped on the bank. Romero planted face first in the dirt. I got up and began fishing for my heel in the murky sludge.

"So graceful," Romero remarked.

"Well, good morning, sleeping beauty. Isn't there anything you'd like to say, hmm? I can take you back if you like."

"In due time. We're not out of the woods yet."

"Bet you're glad you brought me along now, ain't ya? What was that about slowing you down? Deadweight, was it?"

Romero chuckled in the dirt and then groaned.

"Oh, it hurts to laugh."

I pulled my soggy shoe out and wiped it on a rock.

"It serves you right. I told you I could pull my weight."

I put my shoe on and tried to kick off any sand and water. My toes squished in the sludge. Romero struggled to roll himself over. The night atmosphere under the canopy turned cold as night pressed on. We soaked our clothes, wading through the water. My body shivered carrying Romero along.

"There's no point going on," Romero said.

"What do you mean? How can you give up? We're only an hour out, and—"

"Let me finish. We need to set up camp for the night. You'll freeze to death before morning if we don't."

"But I need to protect you, and if they find you, they'll . . . they'll . . ."

"Yes, I know, but let *me* protect *you*. I need to rest. You'll kill yourself if you carry on like this. You're not much good to me dead. We set up camp."

I set him down against a fallen tree. Romero instructed me how to build a fire and gather wood, and then pestered me when I didn't do things "the right way."

Within a little while, a roaring blaze stood before us. Trees surrounded us for miles, and with foggy mists overhead, there was little chance of it being a signal fire. Dense jungle hummed around us. Not another soul for miles. I rested my head on his shoulder, and fireflies began to dance.

"Thank you . . . Sinopa," he said.

"You're welcome. I'm sorry. About before, I mean."

"Don't sweat it, kid. Improv is the ecstasy of show biz. You have to earn your chops for the lead."

Speaking of chops, the cuts on his chest nearly made me vomit. The myst burnt my throat again. I looked at my glove. *How'd Rudolph do it?* I reached over and touched his side. He winced in pain.

"Easy, easy," I hushed him. "Stay still. I'm gonna try something."

The calm of the brook trickled. I remembered the sound of the ocean, how peaceful it was. I remember how at ease I was when Romero and I gazed at the moon earlier. My lungs breathed deep. I exhaled and a coolness formed. My fingers numbed. They began to tingle as if I lost my circulation and the blood was gone.

Romero winced again.

My fingers appeared to gel. They seemed to smooth his skin, spreading it like butter. I breathed in again. My palm pulsated, sending a ripple into his chest. He smacked my hand away.

"Enough," he said. "I'll take the pain before I succumb to your witchcraft."

"I was only trying to h—"

"Well, keep your help to yourself."

His skin appeared to ripple in one bubble in and out of his chest.

In a few moments it slowed, and long scars and plenty of hard scabs formed. My head throbbed again. I thought it to be another migraine as the Jerbalian juice or whatever was leaving my system. *Boy, when Sonia said it speeds up your metabolism, she was right.* That stuff gave me the runs. Like, *bad* runs, and here I was out in the middle of butt-frick-nowhere without a decent latrine. That wasn't fun, let me tell you.

Despite all this, a warm feeling grew inside. This was progress. I was learning. I had become a spell caster. The little girl in me giggled with excitement.

What should I call myself now that I can control the myst? A witch? No, sounds too close to something else I've been called. What about an enchantress?

I liked the sound of that. I was enchanting, wasn't I? Bold enchantress Sinopa the pureblood, the noble bride of Master Rudolph. It had a nice ring to it if you asked me.

My thoughts turned to Rudolph. I wondered where he was. His

company would've been nice right here beside me. He'd been my gallant knight to lend me his sword. His men could surely handle Jasper. Not that I needed him. This enchantress could handle matters all by herself. Thank you very much.

My clothes dried. I felt better but couldn't admit Romero was right, of course. He had enough ego as it was. I begrudgingly apologized for trying to heal him without his permission, as ridiculous a thing as it was. He remained silent. An owl hooted in the distance. Winged silhouettes circled the sky. I remembered Sonia. She was alone, and no one was there to stand up to her captor. I stood up.

Romero looked at me, "Where are you going?"

"I'm going back for Sonia."

"You're crazy. It's suicide. You saw what they did to me. What will happen to you?"

The lump formed in my throat. I couldn't acknowledge how scared I was.

"I made her a promise. Now I'm going back."

"How are you finding her? Do you even know the way back?"

"We traveled in a straight line. It'll be fine. I should be back before the night is over."

I started tracing my steps away from the fire.

"Kid, wait."

"Don't try to stop me."

Romero dug into his jacket pocket. "You'll need this."

His pocket shook as he struggled to pull out the flintlock, *my* flintlock that had paid my passage here. "Best go prepared."

I walked back over to him by the fire.

"I might have tinkered with it a bit since I left that night. The thing's ancient."

"You're giving it back?"

"Well, on loan for the time being. You've got to earn it back, you know."

"And me carrying your skinny hide up them hills wasn't enough?"

"You said it, not me."

I frowned.

"You want it or not? I even already loaded it. All you have to do is cock the hammer and pull the trigger. But you've only got one shot, so make it count."

"You can't spare any ammunition?"

"How are you loading it and where are you carrying it?"

I felt my dress. There were no pockets for the gun. I shoved it down my bra.

"That's where you're carrying it?"

"Why? What's wrong with that?"

"On second thought, you can keep it."

"Oh, come on. I can't be that bad," I teased.

"And touch anything that's been around your slimy scaled iguana sweat sacks? No thanks. A few broken ribs are enough disease for me."

I bent down and squeezed my arms around him.

"Not so tight. I'm still sore," he groaned.

"I won't be long."

"Be careful, kid. I'm rootin' for ya."

CHAPTER TWENTY-EIGHT

Wouldn't you know it—I got lost. Not hopelessly lost, but lost, nonetheless. It took me a moment to retrace my steps. Once I did that, I was golden. Just follow the yellow brick road. Don't worry, Dorothy, I'm coming. Within no time, I stood in the town's square. The streets slept, empty. The frigid breeze blew over me, and the moon, the lonely moon, held itself aloft over the spire behind the Canary Cage.

I looked through the windows from the street. Not a sign of movement, but it was hard to see from this distance. I tried to place my ear against the door to listen inside. The door creaked open.

Stupid horns always getting in the way.

I called out to Sonia quietly.

No response.

I pushed the door open the rest of the way. The oil lantern sat on the counter just like she had left it. All the candles at the tables were still dark. No one was here. Not a good sign.

Please be safe.

I figured maybe she could be waiting for me in my room. I needed to go there anyway to fetch my saber and my boots. There was no way I was coming back here again for it. I removed my heels and tried to tread as lightly as I could. The wood groaned and squeaked, despite my best efforts. I took my key and unlocked my door. As I did so, I found it had been forced open. The lock was broken.

Inside wasn't too promising. Sonia's dresses had been scattered, some were slashed, and strewn across the floor. Bottles of perfume lay overturned or shattered in shards of broken glass across the carpet. The bedsheets stretched forth onto the floor, leaving no stone unturned. Stabbed in the closet door, floating off the ground, was my saber, red with blood.

My arms struggled to pry it free. Whoever stuck it in there did so with some force. I pulled it out and wiped it off with one of the torn ball gowns. I dug through the clothes and found my sheath and belt and fastened them to my waist. There was no time to find my old clothes, but my boots were a must. Whoever invented heels could burn in hell.

I cleaned myself up in the small bowl by the vanity and tied my hair back. This little red bombshell wasn't going down without a fight.

There were only two places left to look: Jasper's room or the basement. The master bedroom meant the chance of bumping into my horrible host. To the basement it was. I climbed down the ladder behind the bar as discreet as possible.

Beneath the building, dampness and decay reeked through the halls. A horrible, foggy myst poured into the basement. My blood began to boil. My throat began to throb. Sweat dripped from my face and I fell to my knees.

Not now. Not now. I'm so close. We don't have time for this.

I tried to cool it like I did for Romero, but the pain was too great. I couldn't concentrate.

Breathe in. Breathe out.

I tried to steady my breathing, grabbing my throat. The myst swarmed around me, clouding my vision. In an instant, I closed my eyes.

The hall glowed in a shade of dull white and gray. I could see. My eyes developed some form of night vision. Where once there had been nothing but wet, foggy darkness, there were details in the stonework and faint images of the hallway beyond the smoky cloud.

My body cooled but my throat remained sore. I picked myself up and continued down the tunnel. My migraine only worsened. I wouldn't know all the side effects of magic till much later. Puberty truly is a terrifying aunt, but sometimes she brings good gifts.

All the torches had been snuffed for the night. I was too curious and, to be honest, a bit terrified to light one. It was like losing a baby tooth for the first time. That's the best way I can describe it.

Down the curtained, barred hallway, I could see once more rows of cells. Only this time, they were lit in full daylight. I could see the outlines of the figures more clearly and their dazzling, mournful eyes in the dark. I promised myself I would free them, every last one.

I came to a cell at the end, on the left. Obscured from my vision in the far corner was a small woman. She seemed familiar. Her hair dangled long and blond. A metal muzzle made for a snout, not a human, caged her nose and mouth. Two gleaming food bowls sat by her head. She was shackled, asleep on the floor, on all fours, with a collar with tags like cattle. It was Cheryl.

I pulled out the key ring I had stolen from Jasper. I fiddled with each one. I even double-checked the ring. Not a single key opened the cell. I kicked the bars. Cheryl groaned. Her eyes opened, and mine locked with hers. Neither of us knew what to say.

I began to cry. I promised her I'd get her out of this. All she had to do was sit tight. And she'd see Simon again, and she'd be okay. All she did was stare at me with hollow eyes. They were empty animal eyes, void of recognition and emotion. All of that had been emptied of her. I had to pry myself from her bars. They'd pay dearly for this.

I assumed, if Sonia was down here, she'd be in the chamber. I came to the iron door and pulled the hatch. I saw a figure with outstretched wings. Rows of dark stripes lined the slit in her dress. I quickly swung open the door.

"Come to gloat some more, dear?" she asked.

"Far from it."

Sonia jumped in surprise. "What are you doing here? Get out of here."

"Not till I get you out of here. I'm keeping my promise."

I began rifling through my keys.

"When he finds you, he's going to kill you," she said, calling out in the dark.

Jasper had gotten smart. These were new locks. None of my keys fit. I started with my bobby pins.

"Suppose I can't let him find me then," I said.

The first lock clinked open. I was starting to get the hang of this. I noticed two long chains dangling from the ceiling, clasping onto Sonia's wings and holding them open. Her left wing, where it had been thick and white, bared blotches of black. A long, bloody slash had clipped her gnarled wing.

I moved over to those next.

"How do you feel?" I asked.

"How do you think?"

The lock released, bringing the wing back to her side.

Sonia sighed. "It's okay. It's not your fault. I just fear—He threatened to use me as bait. He was furious. It wouldn't surprise me if—"

I started the next lock faster. "Guess we better pick up the pace."

Sonia sullenly nodded. "Thank you," she finally choked.

She hobbled to her feet, her back hunched. I could tell she was still in pain.

"Wait, there's something I want to try before we go."

"What is it? We've got to go *now*."

I placed my hand on her side. My mind tried its best to think soothing thoughts. The ocean, the brook in the jungle, my "date," as Romero called it, on the Cornerstone pier overlooking the beach.

My fingers turned numb. My hand went stiff, and the nerves vibrated. Her back pulsated with a dull glow. My eyes adjusted to the light in full color and then things returned to shades of white and gray.

Sonia groaned. I moved my hand over the cuts as I had done for Romero. My fingers sank through her skin, smoothing the creases like sand. A series of roots flashed up in her spine. I pulled my glove away. The glow dulled. The cuts remained intact.

"Did it work?"

She looked at me with a raised eyebrow. "You're a healer?"

I nodded. My head throbbed and my legs buckled.

"Sinopa? Sinopa, get up."

She pulled me to my feet. I felt sick to my stomach. She opened the door and pulled her arm around me. I pulled my arm around her. We supported each other in our crippled states.

"Let's get out of here," she said.

I nodded.

What gives? Why did she still have the cuts?

The rows of cells moaned, calling out to us. I had a bad feeling in the pit of my stomach, and it probably wasn't the booze. We couldn't just leave them. Sonia held me up and I held her. I kept pace and cursed myself for having to leave them. She pushed back the curtain. Halfway free.

But as we rounded the corner, footsteps approached. Jasper descended the cellar stairs with five men in tow. He was different now. His eyes dilated and glowed without pupils.

Torchlight shined by the casks. Men in the back held torches of their own.

"Well, dear sister, so nice of you to join us. Last time you left, I discovered something."

Sonia's wings shot open, shielding me behind her. I could see through the tattered holes in one.

"Ah, Pidge, dear. Good to see even after our little chat your spirit is not broken. How cute."

Sonia's voice was calm and stern. "Let us go now."

"Now, love, that's rude don't you think? She just got here. I mean, besides, we have family matters to discuss."

"You're dead to me, Jasper." Sonia removed her ring and tossed it at his feet.

"Pity. And you were getting so attached to your new sister-in-law, too."

Sonia looked at him and looked at me.

"That's right. Sinopa's a pureblood, too, and she almost slipped right under my nose. If only it hadn't been for your poor little fiancé. There's not a speck of humanity in those bones. Won't Dezzy be sick when I bring in the lost lamb? The high wolf father will be so glad to have you back. Now if you'd be so kind as to step aside."

Sonia raised her wings higher, pushing me toward the taps.

"Always the fighter, Pidge. I like that."

Jasper snapped his fingers.

Sonia screamed, "Run!"

She grabbed my arm. The men rushed. She pulled me close, spread her wings and leapt. We flew a foot, but the torn wing caught no air. We drifted and crashed into a shelf of casks. The large barrels rolled, hitting the men.

Sonia pulled me to my feet. We shot down another row of shelves. Sonia took a hammer and swung. Alcohol poured from the hole in one of the kegs. A frothy brew spewed across the floor. A hyena changeling skidded, smacking into a shelf. Two others tripped over him as they rounded the corner.

"Come on, come on!" Sonia shouted.

We rushed to a door on the far end. As a guard bolted to block our escape, Sonia threw the hammer. It flew end over end, pummeling the guard in the groin. The changeling dropped to his knees with a howl. We barreled inside, slamming the door shut. Sonia held it shut. "You still got those keys?"

"Yeah."

"Well, hurry up, then. Lock the door."

I fumbled with the keys, dropping them under the pressure. Bangs could be heard on the opposite side of the door. The door pulled ajar and then closed. Sonia struggled to hold it shut.

"Well?"

"Which one is it?"

"The brass one."

I looked over the keys.

"They're all brass."

Sonia cursed under her breath. "Gimme those."

She went through the keys one by one. I grabbed the knob and pulled with all my strength. The door pulled harder from the other side. Wrong key.

Shouts came from the outside as more of them were called over. Sonia pushed in another key; no luck. The door shook harder. We could see growling faces outside.

One more key. A large thud slammed into the door. Sonia pushed back harder to regain ground. I turned the key. There was a small metal click. The frame wiggled and shook but didn't budge.

We panted in the tunnel. Sweat dripped from our brows and we slowly came to the same realization.

"We did it," I said, heaving.

"We did it," Sonia said, out of breath.

Then, all at once, it hit her with joy. Her eyes brightened. Her hands grabbed mine, and we began to dance in a circle, leaping.

"Oh my gosh, we did it. We did it. We did it. We did it. We actually did it!"

She pulled me close for a hug. At that moment, the door splintered with a crack. A hand reached through the hole in the door.

"We better get moving," she said.

"Agreed."

My migraine subsided as we walked along the subterranean tunnels. Our voices echoed off the stone walls. A few stalagmites rose from the ground. I pulled Sonia aside so she wouldn't trip over them. I guess I was the only one who could see in the dark.

"What is this place?" I asked.

"The smuggler's cove. It's a series of tunnels and channels that we've used to transport our brew."

"And people?"

Sonia sighed.

"And people. There should be another exit to the blue lotus glades. If we hurry, we'll lose them."

"They won't follow us?"

"There are several exits in these tunnels. We'll just have to gamble that they follow the wrong one. And just to make it more convincing . . ."

She plucked a few feathers with a wince and tossed them at the entrance of one of the tunnels. The place was a labyrinth. The tunnels snaked and interconnected in a massive highway. As we traveled along, we heard an explosion at the far end from where we came. The walls shook.

"What's happening?"

Jasper's voice echoed through the tunnel. "Watch it, you idiots! We need them alive. Block the tunnels. Get the girls. Move!"

The barking of dogs bellowed down the tunnel. I clenched Sonia's hand and pulled her faster through the tunnel. We twisted in and out of tunnels and zig-zagged in any direction away from them. The thumping of footfalls barreled toward us.

We ducked into another tunnel and crouched, still hugging the wall. My heart drummed. I desperately tried to catch my breath. Sonia tried to do the same.

Footsteps came closer. I held my breath. Every sound amplified off the walls. A few wolf changeling men raced forward, howling excitedly. A few others gathered in a clump. The sniffling of snouts puffed by. Torchlight passed the mouth of the tunnels. The barking faded. The world got still.

We got up to move and heard another light set of footsteps.

"Oh Sinopa, Pidge darling, do come out. While I don't relish a chase, you'll have me soil my new shoes. Please come out. I shall not hurt you anymore. You have my word."

The torch flashed down on us in the open.

"There you are."

We barreled down the tunnel.

"Fancy a game of tag, dear sister? The cat and mouse game is more Dezzy's style, not mine. Get it? Ah, you'll get it eventually."

The tunnel was a dead end. Our feet galloped. The rocky ground was hard and slick. I tossed a rock, hoping to send a red herring. We rushed right past Jasper down another cave. He peered his head into the mouth of the cave.

"Peekaboo. I see you." The walls laughed all around us. "You forget, dear sister, I know these tunnels like my own tail. Why cause all this fuss? You're just going to get dirty. I'll be more than happy to draw you a bath before meeting Father, what with our little game."

"You're a monster!" I shouted back.

His feet pattered closer.

Crap!

I could see Jasper smiling in my head. Sonia facepalmed, as I had revealed our hiding spot. She pulled me to my feet and we pressed on.

"Monster? Gee, where have I heard that before? Ah, yes, the humes. They've corrupted you, dear sister. What is all this talk of right and wrong? Good and evil? Your soul needs cleansing. Your mind needs to be opened."

"I will not be brainwashed!"

Sonia thumped me and shook her head. I refused to back down.

"Ouch. Dear sister, that hurts. After all, you just cleansed me. Remember the vial? You finally did what I couldn't. I've been reborn."

My thoughts turned to the broken syringe he'd fallen on.

"Imagine a world, if you will, with no right and wrong. Imagine it. Are you imagining, dear sister? I do hope you will humor me.

"Absolute freedom. No worry or consequence. We are not good or evil, right or wrong. We just are. This is the beautiful world Fenrir showed me.

"Their world believed us animals, and, truly, that is what we are, are we not? Free of worry or consequence. The purebloods were meant to exemplify this cause. Think about it. Picture it, love it, crave it, . . . lust for it.

"We can even be free of such emotions as hate or anger, love or sorrow. We are animals. We don't feel. The entire pack can be viewed as equals. No more shall we be called monsters or vermin."

I called out, "What about Sonia?"

She thumped me again, "Shut up, Sinopa!"

"Surely you must at least have loved her."

"Ah, sister dearest, there you go again. You feel too much and think too little. Yes, at one time I loved her. I loved her more than life itself, but now the transformation is complete. I have no use for emotions."

I looked at Sonia and she shook her head.

"I wanted nothing more than for her to be happy, but then I discovered something. I came here, and we met the order. I was cleansed of my transgressions against the changeling brethren. They coached me over several years how to let go of feelings.

"Certainly it's a hard battle, but surely not impossible, and you don't know how liberating it is. You're drifting untethered and floating like a feather. Sure, I feel some emotions: joy, anger, and curiosity at times, but we all have our vices, do we not?"

We continued down the tunnel.

"The ladder should be somewhere close," Sonia whispered.

The walls narrowed. Dead end. The torchlight floated like a ball that swayed back and forth in the dark. A purple, fanged creature loomed underneath. Two spectral bulbs blinked above a row of teeth. He had little semblance of humanity to us anymore.

Jasper *tsked*.

"Ah, you two live in the dark, do you not? Allow me to show you the light. I do relish having the upper hand. Go ahead change my mind with your . . ." his smile curled further, "feelings."

He laughed in the shadows. There was a faint gold glimmer around his neck. His hand reached and squeezed a dog whistle.

"What about all the people you've hurt? All the people you've abused? Surely you must feel something for them?"

Jasper sighed. "Hate to admit, at times I do. Poor souls can't begin to comprehend the magnitude and riches given to them. But to say 'abused?' Dear sister, do not think of us as monsters."

"You're the monster, not me."

"We kill, eat, and reproduce for our very survival. In fact, if it were up to Northstrand, now, the consul would wipe us off the map. It's a little pruning of the family tree so blooms may result; no harm done. The young must learn."

"What about Cheryl, the magicians—they've done nothing wrong. They live in hiding. They're like us."

Jasper roared, "They are nothing like us!" The whistle's chain broke from his neck. "Those mongrels are worse than humes. Everything is their fault. The High Wolf has told me so. Any bad thing is thrown at us with the mark of the sorcerer. Don't believe me, ask *her*."

I looked at Sonia. She nodded.

"Humes are the real animals to treat us this way. It's the duty of the pureblood to cleanse the earth of them and restore myst to the land. Take your place, Sinopa. Rule with us."

"But with rape and murder? I'll never become like you."

"Pity; you're still not getting it. Such evil is the natural thoughts of humes. Animals like us bear no such fetters. This is nature. So, nudging the next generation into motion and eliminating competition, that's evil? No, it's the way of progress. Perhaps the High Wolf can better explain. Sonia, there's still time. If you were to change your—"

"Drop dead," she shot coldly.

He shrugged and pursed his lips. Like a trumpeter, he blew, raising his head back. There was no sound from the whistle. Jasper's fangs glowed in a tarnished smile. Sonia cursed him and threw a rock, hitting him in the chest.

The creature laughed.

"Am I such a dog that you come at me with sticks and rocks?"

A single, long howl echoed in the distance. One by one, more joined in. Then barking. Sonia frantically threw more rocks at Jasper, standing tall.

"Shan't be long now. Any last words, love?"

I backed up against the wall and felt something hard pinch my skin. My hand flew to my chest and felt the flintlock pressed close to my heart.

CHAPTER TWENTY-NINE

I pulled out the flintlock and cocked the hammer back.

"Let us go. Now," I said, raising the gun.

Jasper's smile faded.

"Do you really know how to shoot that thing?"

I nodded.

"What are you doing? Fire!" Sonia shouted.

"Ah, but then you'd be killing your own brother, would you not?"

"Sinopa, we've got to go. Pull the trigger and let's go."

The gun shook in my hands.

"Ah. Little Miss Morality. Give in to your instincts. Kill, eat, and live. Or perhaps that would make you—oh fancy that!—a murderer."

"Don't listen to him. He deserves this. Kill him! Drop him now."

"I rest my life in your hands, dear sister. I know, whatever you do, it's the right choice."

The hounds howled closer. My finger trembled. The hammer fell back before I pulled the trigger. I cocked it again. Sonia grabbed from behind at my shoulders.

"What are you doing? Fire!"

I screamed. A loud blast bellowed. When I opened my eyes the torch fell. In my night vision, I saw a cloud of smoke, a warm splatter, and a figure fall backward. I collapsed in shock. The blast left a ringing in my ears.

"You're a fool, dear sister. You cannot fight this. You're just like me."

Blood trickled from the corners of his cheeks.

"No, no, I'm not like you."

I brushed the warm liquid from my face. Blood was on my hands.

"Sinopa, let's go," Sonia called from the cloud.

The barking approached, louder and louder.

Jasper's voice rasped with slight gurgles.

"You've proved it right now. I shall become a martyr, and you shall carry my torch. Long live the High Wolf. Long live Fenrir."

I shook my head repeatedly, covering my ears. Jasper coughed with laughter until he fell limp. The cadaver's face plastered itself open with a toothy, fanged grin.

Sonia pulled my shoulder and pried the flintlock from my fingers. Ten feet away stood five changeling men with torches.

"Don't come any closer," Sonia threatened, the gun pointed directly at them.

The group gathered in a clump, bottlenecked from continuing further. As the smoke cleared, eyes turned to the remains of the monster before them.

"Come any closer and you're next."

Sonia flared her wings out and threw me behind her back. I pulled at the saber by my waist. I puffed myself up, too. My body shook like a frightened chihuahua. I felt unsure what to do with the clumsy stick.

The men took a small step back.

"Leave."

The hammer pulled back. An audible click shot through the halls.

"Don't make me ask twice."

The men nodded and whimpered back up the tunnel slowly the way they had come. Sonia grabbed Jasper's torch and we made our way to the small ladder. It had metal rungs like the one we had come down beneath the bar. A heavyset manhole cover blocked the exit. Sonia heaved at it with all her might until the rim rocked loose. She lifted it and pushed it aside. The song of crickets softly pattered above.

Birthed from the sewer hatch, we both fell limp, lying at opposite ends in exhaustion.

"We did it," Sonia cried. "We did it. We're free!"

I lay silently, contemplating the events that had just unfolded. The fading moonlight filtered through the trees. Blood dried on my palms.

I shot a man. I just killed a man. This isn't how things were supposed to happen. There's no way to prove I'm innocent. He's dead.

The city was a place of opportunity. It was my dream, full of wonder and hope. It was a place I was to be accepted with open arms. I should have known it was too good to be true. Here I lay, after fighting for my life, confused.

I got to my feet and started walking. I recognized the brook.

Sonia called out, "Sinopa, where are you going? Sinopa?"

Who am I now? I can't be either Kiera or Sinopa anymore. Surely, I'm something different. They were much too pure, too kind to have done such a thing. Surely, I am a monster.

"Sinopa, wait up, will you, hun?"

Truly, I wanted to stop. I wanted to stop right there, go to sleep, and never wake up again. I approached a small grove of lotus. The lonely moon began to drown itself. I questioned doing the same. I couldn't be like him. Yet, I had killed a man with my bare hands. Dropped him dead on his back. I fell to my knees to wash my hands in the murky brine.

Sonia grabbed my shoulder.

"Hey, what gives? You just kind of stormed off back there."

I scooped up some water for a drink. My lips spat it out.

"He was right, you know. About me, I mean."

"Oh, don't listen to him. He's a wicked man that you need pay no mind."

"Look at me, Sonia."

Blood droplets stained my forehead and cheeks.

"I'm a monster. I . . . I killed a man. I killed my brother. Here I am thinking I would never have a family, and I slaughter the first one I find."

Sonia sat down beside me and began washing her face as well. In the first light of dawn, my eyes caught that her face was bruised, and it became apparent that her wing had been butchered. Mere patches of grisly carnelian feathers remained.

"No real brother of yours would ever do what he did to you. You're a good person, Sinopa. I can tell."

"How can you say that? I put so many people in danger, and . . . and . . ."

"You saved *me*, didn't you?"

Dawn's light forced the suicidal moon beneath the waves. My reflection stood before me in the water. In my horns, my scales, my cat eyes, and tail, I saw only Jasper. Yet I frowned. He smiled.

"You don't want to be like him. Choose not to be. You are who you choose to be."

"I didn't choose to be born this way."

I lashed out my tail. Ripples blotted out my reflection.

"Neither did I. Sometimes we just gotta make the most of the hand we're dealt."

My tail wriggled in anger.

I mocked, "Then who do you choose to be?"

"Come. Sit. I'll show you."

I sighed, dragging my feet back over to the water's edge. The entire basin led into the ocean full of lily pads and white and blue flowers.

"You see these waterlilies? Do you know the story behind them?"

"No, but I suppose you're going to tell it to me anyway."

She ignored me.

"The islands of Jarbah are famous for them. The ancients tell stories of the lotus-eater's isle. People traveling to the island would consume the plant and never leave. They'd be so consumed by the products of the island that they'd never leave. They'd be slaves to the desires they created in themselves."

"So, moral of the story: I will be consumed by bloodlust. Wow, you know . . . just wow. You're not making this any better."

"Think of it this way. Look how pretty these flowers are. They're pretty, right?"

I rolled my eyes. "Get on with it."

"Well, these don't necessarily have the best conditions, either. The shade of the canopy makes it hard to grow. They have little to no soil to root. The waters can be murky and salty. Animals and people come and harvest the petals, and so on. Yet, in these conditions, they flourish and bloom. They produce after their kind and actually end up cleansing the water they live in, over time."

"What's your point?"

"Be a lotus. Be a light in this world. Even though the circumstances are bleak and dark. You can make something beautiful out of this. You can be a lily of this swamp if you choose. That's what I've chosen."

The cricket's song diminished as the moon disappeared. Awkward silence grew between us.

"That was beautiful, Sonia."

"And, if you smoke them, they also get you high as a kite."

We both laughed.

"Thank you, Sonia."

She thumped me on the shoulder and leaned in for a hug. It stung a little bit.

"You're a good person, Sinopa. Don't let anyone tell you otherwise."

The sun rose with dawn's first light. The lonely moon had drowned herself out of sight. It was nice not to be alone. I plucked a lotus flower from the water and placed it in my hair, for good measure. Sonia did the same and smiled at me.

Her eyes were as murky as the water. Funny—we never said it but we thought it. I had lost a brother but gained a sister. Not a sister by blood, or pureblood, or chance, but by love and by choice. I had a sister. It was nice not to be alone.

THANK YOU FOR READING!

Thank you for reading *Vestige: Rise of the Pureblood*! If you enjoyed this story, please leave an honest review on Goodreads or at your favorite retailer where you purchased this novel. It really helps the book do well. Thank you in advance.

Be sure to check out the continuation:
Vestige: What Lies Beneath.
Coming Soon!

You can follow me at

theantonioroberts.com
Goodreads
And on my Facebook author page

www.ingramcontent.com/pod-product-compliance
Lightning Source LLC
Chambersburg PA
CBHW070747180626
46818CB00007B/3025